RICHARD N OSBORNE

YOUNG READERS

Stories of the Diamond

Young Readers Bookshelf

Lantern Press   *The books in the*

YOUNG READERS BOOKSHELF

YOUNG READERS ADVENTURE STORIES
YOUNG READERS AMERICAN FOLK TALES
YOUNG READERS ANIMAL STORIES
YOUNG READERS BASEBALL STORIES
YOUNG READERS BASKETBALL STORIES
YOUNG READERS COWBOY STORIES
YOUNG READERS DETECTIVE STORIES
YOUNG READERS DOG STORIES
YOUNG READERS FOOTBALL STORIES
YOUNG READERS HORSE STORIES
YOUNG READERS INDIAN STORIES
YOUNG READERS INDOOR SPORTS STORIES
YOUNG READERS MYSTERY STORIES
YOUNG READERS OUTDOOR SPORTS STORIES
YOUNG READERS PIONEER STORIES
YOUNG READERS SPORTS STORIES
YOUNG READERS STORIES OF THE DIAMOND
YOUNG READERS STORIES OF HUMOR
YOUNG READERS TREASURY OF SPORTS STORIES
YOUNG READERS WESTERN STORIES
YOUNG READERS WILD LIFE STORIES

YOUNG READERS

Stories of the Diamond

BY CHARLES COOMBS
Author of *Young Readers Baseball Stories,*
Young Readers Football Stories, etc.

ILLUSTRATED BY CHARLES H. GEER

LANTERN PRESS, PUBLISHERS
257 FOURTH AVENUE · NEW YORK 10

PUBLISHED SIMULTANEOUSLY IN CANADA BY
GEORGE J. MC LEOD, LIMITED, TORONTO, ONTARIO
MANUFACTURED IN THE UNITED STATES OF AMERICA

CONTENTS

LIST OF ILLUSTRATIONS

THE PERFECT GAME

Beads of perspiration stood on the tall boy's forehead

THE PERFECT GAME

A flat tire?" Blake Hunter's voice jeered good-naturedly over the telephone. "What have you been doing, riding your bike through the city dump or something?"

Josh Woodford laughed. "Not quite," he

11

said. "Picked up a nail on my paper route last night. Haven't had time to fix it. I . . . I, well, I just thought maybe you'd give me a ride over to the ball park."

Josh couldn't quite figure just why he hesitated in asking Blake. After all, he and the tall, dark-haired boy had been close friends for years. But lately, although neither had mentioned it, things hadn't been just right between them. Oh, nothing you could exactly put your finger on, but it was there just the same . . . a small crack in the solid wall of their friendship.

"Sure," Blake said, "you can ride on my handlebars. But if I get you out in the woods and then lose you, you won't blame me, huh? It would cinch my team winning the game today."

Blake laughed when he said it, but Josh wondered if there wasn't more behind the remark than met the ear. Most of their kidding had been sort of two-edged lately . . . ever since they had found themselves on separate teams in the Hanford City Little League baseball tournament.

Blake rode into the yard about a half-hour later. He was dressed in a red and white Yank uniform. His pitcher's glove dangled from the handlebars. He was whistling, but it was a rather tuneless whistle, as though he was deep in thought. And Blake had plenty to be thoughtful about, too. For today he was due to pitch his big game against the Wildcats. The winning team would be All-City Champs and would get to go to the Little League Regional play-offs in the northern part of the state. Of course, from there it was every Little Leaguer's big dream to go on to the National Tournament at Williamsport, Pennsylvania, home and headquarters of Little League baseball.

"Hi, Blake," Josh came out the back door. His uniform was different from Blake's. It was gray with blue cap, socks and trimmings. It was the Wildcat uniform. He carried his favorite bat over his shoulder.

"Hey," Blake protested, "you might as well leave that bat home today. You're not going to get any hits off of me."

"That's what you think," Josh laughed. "Big boy, I'm going to knock you clear out of the ball park."

"If you do I'll haunt you the rest of your life."

"You don't stand a ghost of a chance," Josh quipped.

Once again the shorter boy detected a sort of strained humor in their banter. As they started toward the Hanford City Little League ball park, he thought back briefly on how the strain in their friendship had come about.

A couple of months ago both he and Blake had been playing for the Yanks. Josh had been the hitting star, and Blake the best pitcher in the league. With the two of them on one team, the Yanks had forged to the top of the league standing early in the season.

Then, since the Little Leagues operate

exactly as do the major leagues . . . except that they play on a two-thirds size diamond and the player age limit is twelve years old . . . Josh was 'sold' to the fourth place Wildcats. Of course, the sale was not made with real money, but by the use of *credits* which each Little League team is given at the first of the season, and which they use for the purpose of 'buying and trading' players.

That was how Blake and he happened to get split up on different teams. And it seemed to have been a good bargain for the Wildcats. Josh's .396 batting average had been a big factor in the Wildcats coming up to the point where they now faced the Yanks in today's play-off for the city title.

"Did you hear how close Mark Lewis came to copping the Garner Trophy the other day?" Josh said by way of starting a conversation. "The Eagles were playing the Blues. Mark held the Blues hitless until the last of the fifth. They only got two hits off of him, at that."

"Yeah," Blake said, "but that's two hits away from the Garner Trophy. Man alive, do you suppose anyone will ever win it?"

Josh didn't answer. Of course, he wasn't a pitcher, and the Garner Trophy was strictly for the hurlers. 'Lefty' Garner, a native son of Hanford City, had been a big star in the major leagues a few years back. As a matter of fact, he had been the only pitcher to throw a no-hit, no-run game in the pennant series. Lefty, not an overly modest man, had figured it as quite a feat. In order to keep the memory of that one game alive, he had donated a very elegant trophy to the Hanford City Little Leagues . . . of which there were three leagues of four teams each. The first player to pitch a no-hit, no-run game was to get the trophy.

So far, except for Mark Lewis's near-miss last week, no one had come close.

Josh wasn't so sure that a trophy like that was very valuable. After all, the pitcher was only one-ninth of a team. And, no matter how you wanted to figure, it just didn't seem right that the pitcher of any team should be out trying to win something for himself . . . instead of for the whole team.

Well, Josh certainly wouldn't begrudge the honor to anyone, though. Still, there didn't seem much to worry about; since the season was drawing to a close, and the Garner Trophy was still on display in the window of the Hanford City *Globe*.

With Josh balanced on the handlebars and Blake doing the pedaling, they soon arrived at the Little League ball park. Quite a crowd of people were there to watch the play-off game. Players from both teams were warming up. The air was filled with the pleasant sounds of baseball and the happy chatter of the players.

"Well," Blake said, as Josh slid off the handlebars and they parked the bike, "this is where friendship ceases."

"Yeah," Josh forced a smile. "Good luck, fellow . . . I hope not."

It was all supposed to be friendly kidding. Yet there was something sort of serious about it. It was something that Josh was afraid of. He certainly didn't want anything to spoil the fun he and Blake had always enjoyed together.

Soon the two teams were warmed up and ready to start the game. The umpire called them together.

"Just so there won't be any arguments about the rules," he said, "let's go over them quickly. First, is everyone here between the ages of 8 and 12?"

Everyone nodded. That was one of the rules of Little League competition. They also knew that no team could have more than five players, age 12, or less than three players age 10 or younger.

They also had their uniforms, which had been furnished by their sponsors. The Wildcats were sponsored by the Rotary Club and the Yanks were backed by the Hanford Department Store.

"All right," the umpire went on, "this is a six inning game, of course. Since we'll call this the Wildcats' home diamond today, the Yanks will go to bat first. Let's have a look at your shoes."

Josh laughed quietly. Most of the fellows wore regular tennis shoes. A few had special tennis type sneakers with rubber cleats molded into the soles. Rubber cleats were allowed, but no metal cleats of any kind.

"All right, boys," the umpire said. "I guess we're ready. You know, of course, that you cannot leave a base until the pitch has reached home plate. Nor may you run on a third strike that is dropped by the catcher. O.K., let's be at it. May the best team win."

The Yanks' lead-off batter started right out with a single over Josh's head into right field.

"Come on, Red," Josh called to the Wildcat pitcher. "Don't let that bother you. Let's double up on them.'

Red smiled. He even looked a little relieved. Sometimes it was an advantage, even

19

this early in the game, for a pitcher to know that he was out of the running for the Garner Trophy. It seemed to help them limber up. Josh had noticed it several times. In fact, it was one reason that he didn't believe dangling such an award in front of the pitcher's nose did the team any good as a whole.

And it worked out this time, too. The next Yank batter worked Red to a three-and-two count, then whiffed a low inside pitch for the third strike.

"That's the old pepper!" Josh yelped happily. "Try it again, Red, old kid."

The next Yank batter swung late at Red's fast pitches. Then he waited out two called balls, and whacked the fifth pitch sharply along the ground toward short stop. The Wildcat infielder raced in, made a running stab at the ball and whipped it to the second baseman for the second out. The keystone sacker pivoted away from the runner's slide and snapped a quick underhand throw toward first. Josh saw it coming in low. He stretched

20

far out, judged the skidding bounce and caught the ball just before the batter's foot touched first base. A double play. The side was retired

"Pretty lucky," Blake said as Josh passed the pitcher's mound on his way to the Wild-cats' dugout. "Watch out next inning."

"You better watch out now," Josh kidded back. "Just pitch that ball and duck fast."

Blake pitched, all right. But he didn't duck. He didn't need to duck. There, in the last half of the first inning, he fanned the lead-off batter with four pitched balls. The second Wildcat batter popped a weak fly to the Yank third baseman. The next man up got tagged on the shoulder by a close pitch. The umpire motioned for him to take first base. But it wasn't chalked up as a hit against the pitcher, so Blake's record was still all right.

Josh, batting in the clean-up spot, picked up his favorite bat and strode to the plate.

"Come on, Josh," his teammates called. "Let's have a homer!"

"Over the fence, Josh!"

The league's leading batter smiled to himself. He gripped the bat with a firm but not extra tight clasp. He looked at his friend, Blake, who stood tight-lipped on the mound. One thing about the tall left hander, he took his pitching seriously. Especially since the Garner Trophy had come into being. Blake never said much about it, but Josh knew that the big hurler figured that if anyone around Hanford would ever pitch a no-hit, no-run game he stood about the best chance of being that one. Blake was a good chucker. There was no getting around that. Although he didn't use it much . . . because he knew that growing boys should stick pretty close to straight pitching and not risk any early strains on the arm . . . Blake could even bend in a nice curve ball when he really wanted to.

The Yank mound ace's first pitch zipped in fast and over the outside corner. Josh swung, and heard the ball plop into the catcher's mitt.

"You looking for this, Josh?" the catcher razzed, holding the ball up for the Wildcat to see; yet keeping a careful eye on the other Wildcat runner on first base.

Josh let the next pitch go by for a called ball. The third pitch was a floater. Josh tried to wait, but he was off balance. He barely ticked it for a foul. Strike two.

"Come on, Josh," his teammate called from first base. "Don't let me die out here!"

Josh planted himself solidly. He sure didn't figure on letting Blake fan him. He watched the next ball speed toward him . . . right over the middle. He started his swing. But the moment the bat was off his shoulder he knew he was cooked. For Blake had pulled the string on a dropping floater. Josh's bat swished over it.

"You're out!" the umpire jerked his thumb up over his shoulder.

Blake left the mound grinning broadly.

"I'll get you next time," Josh promised, as he trotted past Blake on his way out to first base to begin the second inning.

"Not today, pal," the Yanks' southpaw hurler said. "Today I'm really loaded with stuff."

Josh knew what his friend meant. It was apparent in that first inning of pitching that Blake was going to have his big day. Josh had watched each of the pitches . . . excepting

24

the one that hit the Wildcat batter . . . go exactly where Blake wanted it to. Yep, you didn't have to be an expert to know that the Yank pitcher was in for a good day.

And it seemed that Blake's own teammates sensed it, too. "Let's get him a few runs," their first baseman said as he stepped to the plate to start the second inning.

As good as his word, he slammed a long ball into right field. The Wildcat outfielder had to play it off the low fence. By the time the ball was recovered, the Yank hitter had pulled up grinning on second.

With no outs and the runner in scoring position, the Yank coach didn't call for any sacrifice bunts, but let the red-and-white suited players hit away as they wanted.

And how they wanted! By the end of the inning, three Yank runs had crossed home plate.

Just to make it that much worse, Blake set down the next three Wildcat batters in order. No hits, no runs, no errors.

"Man alive," some grown person said from behind the Wildcat dugout. "That boy has really got those Wildcats eating from his hand."

Much as he hated to admit it, Josh had to agree with the fan's remark. Blake really had complete control of the game. It was one of those things that doesn't happen very often. But it was happening today. Blake was unbeatable.

The third inning was the same story . . . no hits, no runs, no errors. Blake fanned Josh for the second time.

"Sorry, pal," the tall pitcher said as his team came in from the field. "But I just can't help myself today. I'm hot as a firecracker."

"You better stay that way," Josh grinned. "Because if I get another turn at bat, I'm going to pickle whatever you throw me."

"Please don't," Blake pleaded, dropping down onto one knee in front of Josh. "Please don't take away my Garner Trophy."

People along the sidelines laughed at the

big pitcher's kidding. But Josh was embarrassed. He didn't like showiness.

"Get up, you goof," he said under his breath.

"Can't take it, huh?" Blake straightened up. "O.K., pal, you asked for it. Next time you get up you won't even see the ball."

27

Josh went on to first base. As he took the warm-up tosses from the infielders, he was suddenly stricken with surprise at the way he and Blake had just traded words. In their years of friendship, they had often razzed each other. But there had never before been the strong overtone of seriousness to it that there had been just a minute ago.

Blake's face had never had that grimness beneath its surface pleasantness. Nor had he, Josh, ever before let Blake's clowning get under his skin.

Things were certainly not right between him and Blake. And Josh felt pretty bum about it. He didn't like the idea of their friendship suddenly ending. Yet, there was no denying it, ever since he had been 'purchased' by the Wildcats, the dark gulf between him and Blake had been widening.

Now it threatened to split wide open.

In the top half of the fourth inning, the Yanks bunched a flurry of hits and scored two more runs.

Yanks 5, Wildcats 0.

With a grimness that wasn't usually part of him, Blake proceeded to shut out the Wild-cats for the fourth consecutive time at bat.

The murmurs from the sidelines became louder and louder as people began to talk about Blake's chances of winning the coveted Garner Trophy.

And it would be his . . . if he could just hold the next six batters hitless. From the way he had been pitching, his chances of doing it were quite good.

Although one Wildcat was walked in the fifth inning, some fancy Yank fielding plus some good pitching on the part of Blake Hunter kept him from getting any further than second base. In fact, no Wildcat runner had gotten beyond second base during the entire game.

Going into the sixth and final inning, Blake still had a no-hit, no-run record. Tension had reached a high point around the Little League ball park.

29

Small thought was given to the question of who would be the victor. Leading by five runs, it was a fair cinch that the Yanks would emerge victorious and represent Hanford City in the regional play-offs.

The big item now was whether or not Blake Hunter would be the one to accomplish the local Little League record of pitching a perfect game . . . and taking home the vaunted Garner Trophy.

To give their pitcher any added confidence he might need, the Yanks pounded home two more runs in the top half of the sixth inning.

Yanks 7, Wildcats 0.

Coming in for their final turn at bat, Josh again walked past the pitcher's mound where Blake was squeezing the small rosin bag to aid his grip on the ball.

"Good luck, Blake," he said. "If you finish off the next three batters, you deserve the Garner Trophy."

Blake looked at him. "I'll finish them, Josh," he said confidently. "I'm not going this far, then muff it at the last minute, you know."

"Maybe . . . and maybe not," Josh said, and went on toward the dugout.

The first Wildcat batter faced Blake with the same futile determination with which the others had faced him all afternoon. And true to form, Blake pitched just five balls. Three of them were strikes, and the subdued Wildcat retreated to the shadows of the dugout.

The second batter did a little better, getting a solid piece of the ball. But, when the Yank second baseman speared out with his glove to drag down the line drive, the result was the same.

Two outs. Last of the sixth inning.

Blake Hunter was within one put-out of the Garner Trophy . . . within one out of his perfect game!

The palms of Josh's hands were moist, as he selected his favorite bat from the pile. He walked slowly to the plate, and squared off with his usual firm stance. Many thoughts

31

were rushing through his head. He didn't look up at Blake. He didn't want to see the expression that might be on his friend's face. Blake might possibly be thinking some of the same things that were going through Josh's own mind.

With two outs in the last inning, and the Yanks leading by seven solid runs, only the dreamiest of day-dreamers would be foolish enough to believe that the Yanks hadn't already won the game.

That was no longer the issue. The issue now was whether Blake could get Josh out. The odds were in his favor. For, although Josh was the leading hitter of the league, Blake Hunter really had his number today. He had fanned Josh twice.

"Batter up," the umpire prompted.

Josh jerked himself out of his thoughts.

"Take it easy, fellow," the Yank catcher said behind him. "You're not going to hit that ball . . . even if you want to."

What did he mean by that 'even if you want to' stuff? Josh wondered. But he knew well enough. In fact, it had been one of the thoughts that kept crowding forward in his mind.

With the game already won by the Yanks, who could do less for a friend about to achieve a great personal victory than just sort of accidentally-on-purpose allow himself to be struck out? He wouldn't even have to do that. He could hit the ball, but not give it quite everything he had. Leave the chance to the Yank fielders. If they muffed it, that was their fault. After all, he would be giving them a fifty-fifty chance to help Blake win his perfect game.

That seemed a cheap enough bargain when friendship was at stake. And it wouldn't cost his own team, the Wildcats, a thing . . . not a single thing. No one was foolish enough to think that they could win the game at this late date.

Yes, it would be a pretty small favor to do for a friend. Maybe this would be just the new boost their slipping friendship needed.

On the other hand, if he spoiled Blake's

perfect game, he and the tall left-hander might be on the outs for good.

"You ready, Josh?" Blake called from the pitcher's mound.

Once more Josh snapped himself out of his thoughts. He crowded up to the plate.

The first pitch came in fast and letter high. Josh watched it go by.

"Strike one!" the umpire called.

"What's the matter, Josh?" someone called. "Those are your meat."

When the Wildcat batsman look up, Blake's face was expressionless. There was no way of telling whether the Yank hurler figured what Josh was thinking.

Josh had presence of mind enough to let the next low pitch go by for a called ball.

He swung viciously over the third pitch for strike two.

And suddenly Josh stepped out of the batter's box and bent down to rub dirt on his sweaty hands. He felt sort of dizzy as a sickening wave of guilt passed through him.

34

Whatever had prompted him to do what he was doing? What kind of friendship could a fellow buy at the price of not doing his best . . . at the price of cheating!

"What's the matter, son?" the umpire asked, looking at him closely. "You're pale. Are you sick?"

"No . . . no sir," Josh said, stepping back into the batter's box. "Not now."

And he wasn't. For he knew now that if Blake finished his perfect game, he would have earned it.

"Watch out, Blake!" he called toward the mound.

Blake had no smile on his face now. Josh could see the beads of perspiration standing out on the tall boy's forehead.

Blake went into his windup. The moment the ball left the pitcher's hand, Josh knew that it had everything on it. He glued his eyes to it, and followed the white blur as it streaked toward the plate.

Josh started his swing. He saw the curve

35

suddenly break inward, and made a last instant adjustment in the arc of his bat.

Crack!

There was no denying the solid impact of Josh's bat on the ball. He dropped the bat and sprinted toward first base.

"Slow down, fellow," the first baseman said. "That ball's still traveling."

Josh glanced up just in time to see the white pellet disappear over the left field fence. But he kept running hard. He was anxious to get off the field. He touched all of the bases, stepped on home plate and kept right on going.

He didn't want to see the look that would surely be on Blake Hunter's face after having his perfect game spoiled at the last possible moment.

As he picked up his glove and started away, Josh didn't even notice the cheering. All he knew was that most everyone was starting toward home. And that was where he wanted to go. He had a lot of thinking to do. He had really ruined things between himself and Blake today. Ruined them good. He kicked viciously at the dirt along the path.

Josh was about two blocks from the park, when a bicycle came skidding up beside him.

"Hey, pal," Blake said, "you were sure in a big hurry to get away. What's the matter? You ashamed of swatting a home run or something? Here, I brought you your bat. You forgot it."

Josh spun around. He looked squarely at Blake, trying to figure out just what the Yank pitcher might be thinking. But all he could see was a genuine smile on Blake's face.

"You . . . you're not sore at me?" Josh asked.

"Sore at you for what?" the tall boy said, surprised.

"For what? For spoiling your no-hit, no-run game, of course."

"What are you talking about?" Blake laughed. "There is no such a thing as a no-hit, no-run game until the last man is out. You didn't spoil it, pal. You just kept it from being. That happens all the time. That's why they're so rare, I guess."

"Boy," Josh glanced down at the ground, "and to think that I almost—"

"You almost loused up a good friendship, pal," Blake looked him straight in the eye. "If I'd ever thought that you were holding back . . . not really doing your best to get that last hit . . . brother, you and I would really have tangled."

"Then we're still friends?" Josh asked.

"What do you mean 'still'?" Blake shoved him playfully. "We've never been anything else. Maybe we get a little excited during a game and stuff. Maybe we even pour it on to each other a little. But, pal, that doesn't bother friends . . . not real friends."

"Boy, how right you are," Josh agreed happily.

"Come on," Blake laughed. "Climb on the handlebars and I'll ride you home."

By the time they reached Josh's house, the

Wildcat slugger had managed to clear all the cobwebs that had gathered in his mind that afternoon.

"Don't worry, Blake," he said. "You'll get that Garner Trophy yet. You're going to pitch a perfect game before the season is over."

"Who cares about the trophy?" Blake said. "If I get it, I'll earn it the hard way. And as for perfect games, what was the matter with today's?"

Josh looked at Blake and smiled. There was no doubting what his friend had in mind. And Josh agreed with it whole-heartedly.

Today they had played the game fairly and squarely. They had given it everything they had.

And that, in anybody's book, is The Perfect Game.

BIG LEAGUE BAT BOY

The star put his arm around the bat boy's shoulder

BIG LEAGUE BAT BOY

Danny Martin was worried as he sorted the bats into the rack near the Falcons' dugout. Usually it was a swell feeling to be bat boy for a big league ball club like the Falcons. Many times during the season he had almost burst with joy and pride when the Falcons had come from behind to win a tough game. One of the big rewards of being a bat boy was to share that feeling of victory after a hard-fought game. Of course, there were other things, too. The splendor of flags around the top of the grandstand. The big crowds. The gay colors. The hot dog and soda pop vendors. The cheering, and the good-natured booing. It was all a part of baseball. Danny loved every minute of it.

At least, almost every minute of it.

Although a bat boy was always supposed to look and act cheerful for the good of the team's morale, it was quite impossible for a good bat boy not to share the team's worries.

And right now the Falcons were plenty worried. Danny could see it in the awkward way they swung at the ball, in the lifeless way they ran the bases and in the uncertain speed and direction of some of their throws. He could tell it in the absence of the fiery chatter that was usually a part of their playing.

Yes, the Falcons were worried. And for good reason. They were in a slump . . . a slump that had lasted for nearly two weeks.

44

And now, in the face of the big play-off series that was to start the next day against the Chiefs, the chances for a Falcon victory seemed gloomier than ever.

"Hey, Danny," Chipper Hanson, Falcon shortstop, called over. "Got a *chaw* with you today?"

Danny knew exactly what Chipper meant. Pushing a grin onto his face, he trotted over and handed the rookie shortstop a stick of bubble gum.

"Good boy," Chipper playfully jerked the visor of Danny's baseball cap down over his eyes. "At least, I can count on you."

"What do you mean, 'at least'?" Danny asked.

"Did I say at least?" the rookie said. "Forget it."

But Danny knew pretty well what the Falcon player meant. Three times during yesterday's game with the Acorns the wiry shortstop had gotten on base . . . twice by hits and once on a walk . . . yet, not once

45

were his teammates able to bat him home. The Falcons had lost another close game.

Chipper had complained afterwards about his teammates being a bunch of dodos who couldn't hit a pumpkin if you put it on a platter in front of them.

Maybe Chipper had been kidding; maybe he hadn't. Danny knew one thing, though. There had been too much of that kind of talk, kidding or otherwise, taking place on the Falcon team. The players just weren't pulling together like they had earlier in the season.

There was something about a team when it got in a slump. The harder they tried, the worse they seemed to get. And pretty soon little arguments began to spring up, which didn't help matters in the least.

As the sports experts put it, the big league Falcons were unraveling at the seams.

"I hoped maybe you would forget the bubble gum," Danny said now. "Costs a penny a stick, you know."

"Why, Danny," Chipper pouted playfully,

"you know I can't do my best without my bubble gum. Besides, I'll pay you back."

"Plenty of hits and no errors tomorrow is plenty of pay for me," Danny said eagerly, as he turned to shag a foul ball.

There was no accounting for some of the strange habits and superstitions that baseball players had. Nor was it up to the bat boy to question them. As a matter of fact, it was part of Danny's job to know the likes and dislikes of each player on the team, and to encourage them wherever it might help to win games.

That was why Danny usually carried an extra stick of bubble gum in his pocket. Childish as it might appear in a big league player, Chipper Hanson just couldn't seem to play his best unless he was munching on a wad of it.

It was pretty much the same idea with center fielders Gene White. Just before he stepped into the batter's box, Gene always bent down, picked up three small pebbles and tossed them over his right shoulder. And sometimes when the area around the batter's box was especially clean, Danny would scatter a few small and harmless pebbles so that Gene would have ammunition for his strange ritual. It was all part of being a bat boy.

Nearly every player had some little trick to perform, or went through some ceremony, or carried some charm intended to help him hit at the plate, or to keep from making errors when out on the field.

Today the ball park was thick with sports writers, photographers, baseball experts and hangers-on of various sorts. Someone said, "How do you think you'll do against Lefty Palmer, Buzz?"

It was a question that was bound to be asked sooner or later. Buzz Benson, the Falcons' leading batter had been carrying a jinx all season. Not once in any of their series with the Chiefs had Buzz been able to hit veteran pitcher Lefty Palmer's fast and tricky throws. And, since without Buzz's help at bat

48

the Falcons wouldn't stand much of a chance in this final pennant series, the local fans were plenty concerned about the jinx.

"Don't worry," Danny piped up loyally in his squeaky voice. "Buzz is going to swat Lefty Palmer's best pitches clear out of the park."

"Yeah, that's right," the husky batter twisted his face into a grin. "Danny's my good luck charm."

"Danny's good luck to all of us," Chipper Nelson said.

"Yes, sir," the others chorused. "Danny's our boy!"

On the outer edge of the circle of people two men glanced at each other. Danny saw them, but he didn't give it any further thought. The two men didn't look like sports writers or photographers. But, then, there were a lot of people who hung around the big league ball parks before a series . . . especially before a big series like the one scheduled to start tomorrow.

49

Besides, Danny was too pleased and proud over the remarks the Falcon players were making about him to worry over two men in dark suits and low-brimmed hats who merely nodded to each other for no apparent reason.

"That's right," one of the newspapermen was saying. "Danny fixed up a bat for you or something, didn't he, Buzz?"

"Sure did," Buzz said. "Show it to them, Danny."

The twelve year old bat boy went over and got a sturdy bat from the rack. He held it with pride. He had spent many hours at home working on that bat. For his large husky frame, Buzz Benson had small hands. Danny had worked hard hand-sanding the bat handle down to fit comfortably in the star hitter's grip. Then he had bone-rubbed it until its tan surface was hard and glistening.

"But you haven't been getting any hits lately," the newsman reminded. "How come, Buzz, if that bat's so lucky?"

"It got lost," Buzz said. "I didn't have it

all during that last series with the Acorns. I just got it back again last night. Danny located it."

What Buzz didn't know was that the bat the newspaperman was now looking at was not the same bat that had disappeared a week or so ago. The first one which had so mysteriously turned up missing just before the series with the Acorns had never been found. This was a duplicate, as close as Danny had been able to fix it up to look like the other one.

It had been Mort Gaines' idea. And only Danny and the Falcon manager knew about the second bat. As Mr. Gaines had said, "Luck is pretty much in the player's mind, Danny. So as long as Buzz doesn't know that this isn't the original lucky bat, it won't make much difference. You better take care of it yourself, though, so that it won't get lost like the other one."

More than once Danny had wondered if the first bat had really been lost, or if something else had happened to it.

"Well, don't you fellows go placing any bets on the Falcons winning the series," someone said.

"Let's cut out any of that kind of gambling talk around here," Mort Gaines spoke up sharply.

Danny remembered hearing his father read in the paper about how some gamblers who had come to town for the series were making large bets against the Falcons. It was strictly unlawful and the police were trying to catch the men.

It made Danny mad even to hear about it. Baseball was a great game. And to think of greedy crooks trying to ruin it by using it for purposes of gambling . . . well, it just made the young bat boy's blood boil.

For the next half hour Danny shagged foul balls as the Falcons took their practice turns at bat.

"All right, fellows," Manager Gaines called. "That's enough for today. Take a couple laps around the park and get your showers. And

52

when you arrive here tomorrow, come with the idea of winning that first game. If we lose it our pennant chances are just about shot."

While the Falcons were taking their laps around the field, Danny quickly gathered up the balls, put the bats in the bat bags, locked the catcher's chest protector, shin guards and mask in the dugout locker, and did the various other little chores that were part of the bat boy's job.

Then he hurried down into the locker room to hand out the towels as the players came out of the showers.

But Danny had kept one bat out of the bags. He wasn't going to take any chances of having it turn up missing like the first one. Lefty Palmer was going to pitch tomorrow's series opener, and Buzz Benson would need that bat.

No one was looking when Danny put it in the locker that he used for his own stuff, and spun the combination.

By the time he had picked up the towels

and straightened up the locker room, Danny's day as bat boy had ended.

"See you tomorrow, son," Mort Gaines

called through the open door of his office as Danny started up the stairs toward home. "I'm going to count on you out there tomorrow, Danny. You know a lot of the little tricks it takes to make those guys play their best ball. Work the game hard tomorrow, won't you? We sure need the victory."

"I'll sure do my best, Mr. Gaines," Danny promised. It was a pretty good feeling to be able to think that even the manager counted on the bat boy to help win games. "And we'll win, all right."

He went on up the stairs whistling. But the whistle sort of faded out at times when he recalled how ragged some of the players had looked in that afternoon's practice. They certainly hadn't shown many signs of coming out of their slump.

The following morning was bright and sunny. A slight breeze was blowing from the south, helping to cool the air. It was going to be an ideal day for the first game of the series.

It was a quarter to twelve when Danny finished up his chores and was ready to leave for the ball park. He ate a sandwich, drank a large glass of milk and hurried out to the garage to get his bike. He moaned when he saw it. The head of a tack stuck up through the rubber. The tire was flat.

"I'll just have to run for it," he told his mother. "I'm already a little late. Sure don't have time to take the tire off and patch the tube."

"Now, don't wear yourself out in this hot weather, son," his mother cautioned. "The team will be able to get along for a little while without you."

Danny didn't argue. Most people didn't realize just how important the bat boy was to a team. Hadn't even Mort Gaines said that he was counting on him to help win today's game?

The ball park was nearly two miles from Danny's house. He started off at an easy lope down Lake Street. He didn't notice the dark sedan with the two men in it that started following him almost as soon as he left his house.

He had gone less than two blocks when the car drove up beside him.

"Hi, kid," a fat man behind the wheel said. "Where's the fire?"

Danny slowed down. It seemed he had seen the two men before.

"No fire," he panted slightly. "I've got to get down to the ball park. I'm bat boy for the Falcons."

"You are?" the man nearest the curb said. "Well, ain't that lucky. You see, we're Falcon fans ourselves. Happen to be on our way to the game, too. Hop in. We'll give you a lift."

But Danny still hadn't been able to place the men. And he certainly wasn't going to get into any car with strangers.

"Thanks, anyway," he said. "But I'll make it all right on foot."

"Well, have it your way," the heavy-set man said. "We just thought maybe you would like to be with us when we give Buzz Benson his lucky bat."

Danny stopped suddenly, and the car came to a halt at the curb beside him.

"What lucky bat?" Danny said.

"Why, this one, of course," the smaller man held it up. "We found it."

Danny saw in a jiffy that it was the first bat he had fixed for Buzz . . . the one that had disappeared so mysteriously.

"Where . . . where did you get it?" he asked.

"It's like I said—we found it."

"We sure hope Buzz will wallop the ball with it today," the fat one said.

"Well, we don't want to miss any of the game," his smaller companion added. "Sorry you won't ride with us, kid. The Falcons may not like the idea of your being late. It's nearly time for the game to start, you know."

About that time Danny remembered where he had seen the men. They were the two who had been at the ball park yesterday. The two who had nodded at each other when the Falcons were bragging to the newsmen just how much they counted on Danny for their luck. No doubt these two men were telling the truth about being loyal Falcon fans. Besides, didn't they say that they were taking the bat to Buzz? Now Danny was glad that he had hidden the second one in his locker yesterday afternoon. He'd leave it there, and Buzz wouldn't realize that there had been two of the lucky bats.

"I . . . I guess I'll ride to the park with you, at that," Danny changed his mind.

"Now you're getting smart," the fat man said. "Hop in."

They had gone about two blocks when the driver turned off Lake Street.

"Hey," Danny protested, "this isn't the way to the ball park."

"Got to pick up a friend," the skinny man who hemmed him in on his right said. "Just relax, kid."

Danny didn't like the sudden change that had come into the man's voice. The friendliness seemed to have gone out of it.

"Hey, let me out," Danny said anxiously. "I'd rather walk."

"Just sit tight, kid," the big man said. "Just

sit tight and keep quiet, and you won't get hurt." He turned the car off the paved street and they wound along a lonely dirt road through the woods that bordered the city. They were just a block or so off the highway when the big car coughed to a stop. "Hm-m," the driver said. "Something must have gone wrong."

But although Danny had been looking out the window with alarm, out of the corner of his eye he had seen the man reach down quickly and switch off the ignition. Now the bat boy was really frightened.

"That's sure tough luck," the small man chuckled. "Must be out of gas or something."

Fear got a firm grip on Danny, deep down inside.

"You . . . you men aren't Falcon fans!" he accused.

The skinny one laughed. "We're fans when the Falcons are losing," he said. "And they've got to lose today."

"Don't talk so much!" the driver snapped at his companion.

60

But Danny had heard enough to figure out what it was all about. These two men were the gamblers that the police were trying to find. Probably they had bet a lot of money on the Chiefs to win.

"But . . . but why are you kidnapping me?" Danny asked, looking around to see if there was any way he might escape . . . and finding none.

"Who's kidnapping?" the fat man said gruffly. "We were just giving you a ride, and we ran out of gas."

"That's not so," Danny cried. "I saw you turn off the key."

"You just thought you saw," the small man said. "Turn on the car radio, Moose. The game ought to be starting."

Many thoughts swirled through Danny's head as he sat between the two men and listened to the radio announcer giving the lineups of the teams.

" '. . . just a minute, fans,' " the announcer went on. " 'There seems to be lot of excitement around the Falcons' dugout.

Someone just handed me a note. Great guns, Danny Martin, the Falcons' bat boy and good luck piece seems to be missing. Yes sir, ladies and gentlemen, there's a lot of confusion around the Falcons' dugout. In case you people don't know it, a bat boy is a very important member of any team. The Falcons count a lot on little Danny Martin. Unless Danny shows up pretty quick, this might just be the bad turn of luck that will spell defeat . . . and a very costly defeat, ladies and gentlemen . . . for the Falcons.' "

Danny stiffened in his seat.

"You . . . you crooks stole that bat of Buzz's, too," he accused. "You probably were betting against us in the series with the Acorns, too."

The skinny fellow laughed. "Could be," he admitted. "And you just never know what little thing is liable to ruin a team's game."

"Yeah, even a little thing like having your car break down just when you're giving their bat boy a lift to the game," the fat man was getting more talkative. "Sure is tough if they don't have their luck with them today."

Danny sat silently and pretended to be listening to the radio. He heard enough to know that the Falcons were three runs behind by the end of the second inning. But his main thoughts were on how he might be able to escape from the two crooks who sat on each side of him.

"Looks like easy money today," the skinny man chuckled.

No doubt, if the Falcons lost the game, the two men would quickly collect their money and leave town. Danny's father had said that gamblers move around fast, and are mighty hard to catch. Of course, he had added, people who are foolish enough to gamble with such men deserve to lose their money. But if you could catch the men at the bottom of it, the whole thing would be stopped.

And Danny felt sure that these were the two men at the bottom.

Once Danny tried to jump over into the

63

back seat and out the door. But the skinny man was too quick for him.

"Look, kid," he warned, as he jerked the bat boy back into the front seat. "We don't want to hurt you any. So just sit still and listen to your Falcons get beat. As soon as the game's over, you can go home and nobody's any the worse off. The Falcons would probably lose today, even if you were there."

"Then why are you holding me?" Danny held back a sob.

"Like I said—we just ran out of gas."

"There's a service station right behind us on the highway," Danny challenged.

"Just pipe down and listen to the game," the man called Moose said.

It was the last of the fifth inning and the Chiefs were leading by a score of 6 to 2. Buzz had failed to get a single hit off of Lefty Palmer. Danny remembered numbly that he had put the star hitter's lucky bat away in his locker the day before. Other Falcon players were making errors on the field, and Danny

64

wondered whether Chipper had his stick of bubble gum, and whether Gene White had found any pebbles to pick up.

They were all the little things that were hidden, yet very important parts of any ball game to the Falcons.

Danny crowded back helpless tears.

"Let me go," he pleaded.

"It won't be long now," the fat man said.

"I'm out of cigarettes," the other patted his pockets. "Think I'll walk back to that stand on the highway and get some. Keep an eye on the kid."

He wasn't gone more than two minutes, when Danny suddenly saw the chance he had been waiting for. The sun had been getting lower and lower until now it came in under the car top and fell across the big gambler's face. When he reached up to pull down one of the visors, his arm and shoulder cut out his view of Danny for just a moment.

But Danny was prepared. In that brief moment when the gambler was offguard,

65

Danny kicked out hard at the man's exposed right shin. Almost at the same moment, he grabbed the keys out of the dashboard with his left hand and jerked down on the door handle with his right.

The big man let out a pained bellow and grabbed for the bat boy. But the door had swung open, and Danny hit the ground running. He plunged into the woods beside the road and kept going. For a few frantic minutes he heard the gambler's labored breathing right behind him. Then it died away and Danny was alone crashing through the thick undergrowth in the general direction of the highway.

When he finally stumbled onto the pavement, he was scratched and bleeding and completely breathless. He stopped just long enough to get his bearings, then plunged on in the direction of the ball park. He had gone a block or so when a black-and-white police prowl car pulled up beside him.

"Hey, pal," the policeman said. "What are you running away from? How come the scratches and . . . say, aren't you Danny Martin?"

"I . . . I've got to get to the ball park!" Danny gasped.

"You're Danny, all right. We've been looking all over for you. What happened?"

Words began to pour out of the bat boy

in gasping sentences. He was hardly conscious of the fact that the policeman was talking through his two-way car radio just about as fast as Danny was telling him his story.

"Don't worry, kid," the policeman said a moment later. "I've got all the other cars in the district converging on those crooks. Besides, they're not going any place as long as you have the keys to their car. You did a good job, Danny. The police have been after that pair for a long time. Come on. Jump in. From the last score I heard, the Falcons can use some help. Maybe you're just the one who can give it to them. Don't mind riding behind a siren, do you?"

"No siree!" Danny climbed into the police car and they sped away, as the siren wailed, opening a path for them.

The score was 7 to 3 in favor of the Chiefs when Danny ran down the aisle of the grandstand, vaulted over the infield fence and rushed toward the Falcon dugout. The Falcons were just coming in for their seventh turn at bat.

68

"Danny!" Buzz Benson grabbed him. "Where have you been? Where's my bat? Who . . . how—"

"Take it easy, Buzz," Manager Gaines cut in. "Danny looks like he's had some trouble. O.K., son, just what happened?"

For the second time in the last fifteen minutes, Danny quickly told his story. He saw the angry expressions move onto the Falcons' faces.

"Why, those crooks!" Gene White snapped. "Boy, if I could just get my hands on them!"

"How about getting your hands on a bat?" the umpire stuck his head into the dugout. "This is a ball game. Remember? You can serve tea and cake later."

"Here, Gene," Danny cried, running to the rack and getting the outfielder's favorite bat. "And don't forget to pick up your pebbles, huh?"

"Forgot all about it last time," Gene said. He tossed his pebbles, stepped up to the plate and whammed the third pitch for a two-base hit.

Mort Gaines said, "Now let's see the rest of you guys keep the game alive."

"I'll get your bat, Buzz," Danny said. "I hid it in my locker yesterday so that no one would steal it this time."

"I know it's not the same one you fixed for me first, kid," Buzz grinned. "But that's O.K. You're my luck today, Danny."

And just to prove it, Buzz took the bat, worked Lefty Palmer to a full three-and-two count, then smacked the big pitch clear over the left field wall.

Danny met him gleefully at the plate as Buzz trotted across with his home run. The star batter rumpled Danny's hair playfully and put his arm around the bat boy's shoulders as they walked together to the dugout.

"It's sure good to have you back with us, kid," he said.

By the time the seventh inning ended, the Falcons had closed the score up, and were behind by only one run; 7 to 6.

"We'll get this game for you, Danny,"

Chipper promised, as the bat boy dug into his pocket and handed the shortstop the usual stick of bubble gum.

"Sure we will," one of the other players chimed in. "Those gamblers aren't only going to jail, but are going to lose all of their money, to boot."

Danny busied himself re-arranging the bats in the rack just the way each player seemed to want his. Then he checked the cups at the water cooler, dug out a new rosin bag for the batters and did a dozen other little things that are all part of a bat boy's job.

It was while he was breaking open a new box of balls for the umpire that Mort Gaines came over to him. "I think they've found it finally, Danny. Take a peek out there. Those guys are looking like a ball team again."

"What have they found, Mr. Gaines?" Danny asked. But he also could see the change that had come over the team.

"Why, they've found something to take their minds off the slump, Danny," the manager explained. "They were beating themselves, you know. In their own minds. Worrying all the time. Those team slumps are mighty tough things to whip once they get hold of you. I've seen it happen many times. But once they get over the hump . . . well, just watch out."

"Are they over the hump now, Mr. Gaines?" Danny asked.

"Don't they look it?"

"I . . . I guess so," Danny said.

"What I mean, son," the manager went on, "is that they've got you on their minds now. And they're thinking of the dirty trick those gamblers tried to pull. Imagine being so low as to kidnap the bat boy. But crooks like that will try anything to turn the tide in their favor. It's enough to make anybody good and sore."

"Is the team angry, do you think, Mr. Gaines?" Danny asked.

"Just angry enough to play good ball,

72

Danny. And that's just what we needed, I guess."

Well, it was certainly true that the Falcons looked like a different team. Played like it, too. They fielded the ball with a sure-handedness that had been missing for quite some time. They put the Chiefs down in rapid order in the first half of the eighth inning.

"O.K., Danny," Chipper said as he took the bat Danny handed him to start the final half of the eighth. "This one's in payment for the bubble gum."

Then, instead of smacking a line drive, which was Chipper's specialty, the little shortstop crossed up the Chiefs' infield by bunting the first pitch down the third base line and beating out the throw to first. That seemed to wipe some of the smiles off the Chiefs' faces. The next batter sacrificed Chipper to second base.

With one away, Gil Landers, Falcon third baseman, popped a Texas-league single over

73

the second baseman's head. Chipper scampered home with the tieing run, while the Falcon rooters yelled themselves hoarse.

The Chiefs were able to hold them to the tie as the inning ended.

The first of the ninth went quickly. Gene White practically climbed to the top of the center field wall to snag a long fly that looked good for extra bases. One out. A few minutes later, with a runner on first base, Chipper Nelson speared a scorching line drive right off of his shoestrings, whirled and pegged to first base for a double out.

The last half of the ninth. Score tied 7 to 7.

But the Chiefs were far from giving up. Lefty Palmer was able to fan the first Falcon batter.

"Sorry, Danny," the infielder apologized when he handed the bat boy his stick. "I tried."

"No one can hit them all, Bob," Danny grinned.

The next batter got a single, but stayed

74

right on first base when the Chief catcher trapped a high foul just before it hit the screen behind home plate.

With two outs and a runner on first, Buzz Benson took the bat Danny handed him.

"This one is for a certain bat boy I know, Danny," Buzz smiled. "And a mighty hard-working and loyal kid, to boot."

Danny blushed.

But just to prove he meant what he said, Buzz strode to the plate brandishing his favorite bat.

"Watch out, Lefty," he called toward the mound. Danny grinned and saw the pleased look on Mort Gaines' face. That sounded just like the Buzz Benson of old.

And it must have been the old Buzz, too. For he swung into the third pitch with all his might. The crack of bat on ball echoed through the ball park. The white pellet arched high into the blue sky. It wasn't a home run . . . not quite. But by the time the Chief's left fielder played the rebound off the wall and got his throw headed homeward, the Falcon run had crossed the plate.

The Falcons won. 8 to 7.

It had been a long time since Danny had seen the Falcon players so happy. It was as though they knew that their slump was ended. No more jinxes. It even seemed to make them sort of wild.

At least, Danny figured they were wild. What other reason could there be for a big league team to hoist the bat boy onto their shoulders and start parading around the ball park?

Sure they were wild . . . wild with a new happiness. But it didn't frighten Danny so very much.

In fact, it was all pretty wonderful!

YOU JUST
NEVER KNOW

The ball plopped into the catcher's mitt

YOU JUST NEVER KNOW

Choke up on that bat," the voice called from the sidelines. "That chucker's been burning 'em right past you like a bucket of hot rivets."

Barry Parker stood squared away at the plate. From where I squatted waiting my turn at bat, I could see Barry's ears slowly turn crimson. That same squeaky voice had been keeping up a steady barrage of advice ever since the game started. And now, in the last half of the third inning, with the Wheatville Huskers leading us 4 to 2, the voice was becoming too irritating for comfort. After all, this was a big game in the Valley Championship Summer League.

To make matters worse, that voice belonged to a girl . . . a girl who seemed to think she could tell us how to play baseball.

I swung around and scowled at her. She was taffy-haired, had bright blue eyes, and a slightly upturned nose which was splattered with freckles.

"Look, kid," I said, "how about putting a muffler on that foghorn of yours?"

She didn't seem to like that 'kid' stuff so much. Actually, she couldn't have been more than a year younger than I was. Little sparks began to flicker in her sharp eyes. "This is a public playground," she said simply. "I can yell just as much as I want. But I'm beginning to think it'll take a lot more than shouting to make a team out of you fellows."

Some of the spectators nearby began to laugh.

"Oh, we can do very nicely without your coaching," I insisted stubbornly. Although some of the playground teams from other towns had summer coaches, Valley Center didn't. After all, we were just a small town of eight hundred and sixty people, plus about fifty dogs. We didn't rate a lot of the things that the teams from bigger cities did.

"It doesn't exactly look as though you're doing so well without any coaching," she nodded toward the scoreboard.

"Well, if you've got to root," I said, ignoring her accurate remark, "try doing it for Wheatville."

"Valley Center's my home," she said.

Well, of course it was true. Although she had arrived at Valley Center just a couple of weeks before school was out, I guess anyone who moves to a new place has the right to

81

call it her home. As I recalled, her name was Sally Morgan. I believe her folks had bought the old Medford farm a couple of miles west of town.

Paying no heed to Sally's earlier words, Barry clutched the bat clear back on the knob. The Husker pitcher wound up and let fly. Barry swung viciously at the pitch. The ball zipped past him and plopped into the catcher's mitt before Barry even had his swing well under way.

"Batter out!" the umpire called.

"What'd I tell you?" Sally shouted. "That pitcher's got too much speed on the ball for a heavy bat like that."

I gulped and looked away guiltily. Frankly, I had wanted to tell Barry to choke up on his bat, too. But Sally had beaten me to it, and . . . well, I wasn't going to take baseball advice from any girl. Neither was Barry, nor Brick, nor Ziggy, nor any of the other Valley Center Hawks. Baseball is a man's game.

I was really sizzling around my collar when I stepped up to the plate.

"Pull one along the left field baseline," she called again, just loud enough to reach my ears. "There's a whole cow pasture out there."

Even if I had had any idea of doing it, which I'm not sure I did, her unwelcome advice would have changed my mind. The Husker pitcher's throw came floating in towards the plate like a blimp on a string. I had plenty of time to figure out what to do with it. I purposely swung a split second late. The ball sailed into deep center . . . right into the waiting fielder's hands.

That very same hit, pulled down the left field baseline would have been good for extra bases. As I started toward the pitcher's box for the first half of the fourth, I couldn't help but notice our self-appointed coach shaking her head sadly.

The first Husker batter strode up to the plate.

"Give it to him close!" she shouted. "Dust him off, Teddy!"

Naturally . . . just as you would do if a girl was telling you how to play baseball . . .

I pitched him a wide one. There was an enormous "crack!". The ball was still going the other way when the Husker hitter crossed home plate with that home-run grin spread across his pan.

Sally gave me one of those I-told-you-so looks. I called time out and strode over to her. "Look," I growled, "what will you take to go home where you belong?"

"Oh, I like ball games," she said. "Only I like good ball games better than this." She looked me right smack in the eyes.

"Oh, you do?" I buttered my words with a thick spread of sarcasm.

"Yes, I really do."

"Now, see here, Sally," I said, slowed down a little by her quick spunk. "Don't you know that this is a regular championship game?"

"I most certainly do," she said. "All the more reason why you guys should use your heads. Baseball isn't all with the hands and feet, you know."

"Wow!" I wowed. "Some talk for a girl. You ought to write a book."

84

"Play ball!" the umpire called impatiently.

Well, Sally kept right on yelping at us as though she had been elected official coach for the Valley Center Hawks or something.

And we kept doing just the opposite to what she said. Why, taking advice from a girl in matters of baseball could . . . could maybe ruin the world of sports.

But at the beginning of the sixth inning, with the Huskers leading 7 runs to 3, we were getting desperate. Since the summer league games were only seven innings long, time was running out. Barry Parker came over from first base as I stepped to the pitcher's mound.

"Ted," he said, hardly daring to look at me. "Th—that Sally has been calling things awfully close, hasn't she? Maybe it wouldn't really hurt to test her system."

"Barry!" I yelped. "Are you going to take the word of a girl, and . . . well, we might try it, at that." Frankly, I had been thinking much the same thing, but I sure wasn't anxious to admit it.

But now there was a strange silence from the

sidelines. Glancing over slyly, I saw that Sally had a sort of hurt look on her face. Oh, she was trying to hide it as best she could. But, well, I guess I had been kind of tough on her.

O.K., then, let her pout. Maybe it was better that way. I settled down for some really hot and fancy pitching. It probably would have worked, too . . . except that the first two Husker batters got good solid hits.

Then I about sank through the ground when I saw the Husker's hardest hitting batter step up to the plate. It was a cinch that if they scored any more runs it would take a miracle to beat them.

"O.K., Sally," I taunted. "What does the girl master mind say to do now?" I tried to make it sound like I was razzing her. Actually, I'm afraid that I was at a real loss to know what to do. That slugger had whammed everything I had sent his way all afternoon.

Sally glanced up. There was a mixture of defiance and willingness to help in her eyes. "If you must know," she said. "He's a pigeon for them high and inside."

I looked over at Barry. He just shrugged. Then I saw the worried look on the Husker's face, as though maybe he wished Sally hadn't brought up the subject of high inside pitches.

The first pitch was too high. Ball one. The second one went in armpit high and over the inside corner. The Husker batter swung viciously.

Crack! It was a weak pop-up . . . right into Brick Rolland's waiting glove.

Well, we looked at each other; then over to Sally. But Sally wasn't there. I saw her heading down the dirt road towards home.

"Time out!" I called, and raced after her.

I didn't take long to find out that a girl with a made-up mind is no easy problem to tackle.

"You seemed quite certain that you didn't want any girls meddling in your ball games," she said. "So if you don't mind, I'll go on home where I'm appreciated."

Well, I wasn't above a certain amount of wheedling. And finally I led her back to the game. She protested, but weakly.

As soon as we had the third out, I called the Hawks together. "Look, guys," I said nobly, "treat Sally right, huh? She's our . . . our, well, sort of lucky charm."

"You're wrong again, Teddy," she said matter-of-factly, as though I was usually wrong. "Playing ball isn't luck."

"Sure, sure," I blushed, I didn't want to disagree and have her run out on us again. Not after figuring that Husker batter the way she did. "Here, Sally, how about sitting here on our bench? Give her a seat, Ziggy. Where are your manners?"

88

Sally sat down and seemed to size up the situation each time one of us went to bat. She always seemed to know just what to do. As she whispered her ideas, I quickly passed them on to each batter as he stepped up to the plate to take his cuts.

I began to realize that Sally was a very strange person. She seemed to know an awful lot about baseball, even for a boy . . . which, of course, she wasn't. It was all very peculiar.

But when two Hawk runs crossed home plate to bring the score up to Huskers 7, Hawks 5, it wouldn't have mattered if she had had three legs and an eye in the middle of her forehead. We would still have been sold on Sally Morgan. She always seemed to know just what was best.

Under her careful coaching we were able to put the Huskers down in their half of the seventh and last inning. We went in to our last bats still trailing by two runs. We were jumpier than fleas on a hot stove. This game meant plenty. For three straight years the Wheatville Huskers had made us eat diamond crow.

Brick blooped a Texas leaguer over second base for a single. He went to second on a fielder's choice. Ziggy poled a long fly into deep right. Brick tagged up and advanced to third after the catch.

"Drag one down the left field line," Sally said softly as Pete Lawrence picked up a bat. I looked and, sure enough, there was a whole vacant cow pasture out there. The left fielder had failed to move back over, after Ziggy, a southpaw, had pulled him almost over into center field.

If Pete could only lift one over the third baseman's head.

I passed the word quickly to Pete. He stepped into the first pitch. There was no altitude to the hit, but it was hard enough so that it went right past the third baseman. Brick scored easily. Pete stretched the hit into a two-bagger. We trailed 7 to 6. Two outs.

Barry was our hardest hitter. Although it isn't usually a good idea to put the possible winning run on base, the Husker pitcher decided to walk Barry. Now any base except home plate was a force out base.

I got up to take my turn at bat. All the worries of the world were on my shoulders. Frankly, I was too scared even to think straight about what I should do. This was really what you'd call batting in the clutch. I glanced over at Sally. My face must have had about as much expression as a paper plate.

Sally smiled. "Teddy," she said, "we've got to get Pete to third. Just swing at the first pitch. No matter where it is. But don't hit it!"

I was too numb to argue. Or to notice the sly signal she gave Pete on second. The first pitch was practically in the dirt. I was sorely tempted to let it go by. But that little voice . . . that little feminine voice . . . kept prodding me. I swung. I missed by a country mile. But my swinging was just enough to make the Husker catcher bobble the ball a moment. During that moment Pete raced to third, making it in a cloud of dust.

Well, that bit of strategy made Sally the fair-haired girl for sure! If we could bring in that one tieing run, I wasn't worried about winning the game in extra innings. Not with Sally there.

"Teddy," Sally beckoned to me. And far be it from me to ignore her beck, especially after that last stroke of genius.

But even genius can go astray. And what she told me when I went over was a perfect indication that genius was straying at that moment.

"Sally!" I protested. "That would be crazy! There are two outs and . . . and—"

She just shrugged. "Suit yourself," she said. "It was merely an idea. I've seen games won by doing it, though. I've even seen Ted Williams do it."

"You've seen Ted Williams!" I challenged. "Boy, you sure talk like a big leaguer."

"You're getting warm," she grinned.

What a gal!

Well, I stepped back in the batter's box. My knees were trembling like an alder branch in a high wind. The next pitch came in fast. Though I hadn't intended to do it, I made up my mind in a split second. As the ball sped toward me, I slid one hand out along the bat, faced the pitcher and laid a bunt right down the third base line.

With two outs the Huskers, playing fairly

93

deep, were caught flat-footed. Pete hopped over the ball coming into home. I was on first base two full steps ahead of the third baseman's throw.

The score was tied.

That bunt really seemed to have taken the starch out of the Husker team. The pitcher was fit to be tied. In fact, he made the big mistake of grooving the next pitch to Manny Weaver . . . which Manny smacked clear into the next county.

As Barry crossed home plate with the winning run, the rest of us swarmed down on Sally. The questions began to fly thick and fast. Sally sat and took it all smiling.

"You can't live around baseball players all your life," she said, "without picking up a few pointers, whether you want to or not. And it doesn't matter whether you're a girl or a boy."

"Live around players?" I said. "Does your father, or your brother, or—"

94

"My brother," she said matter-of-factly.

"Where?" Manny asked.

"Philadelphia."

Barry gasped. "You . . . you mean big league?"

Morgan. Morgan? Philadelphia. I began thumbing through my mental catalogue of big league players. What player by the name of Morgan played for Phil—"

"Sally!" I shouted. "Not . . . not Bobo Morgan?"

"Sure. Why not?" she smiled. "He likes having a little sister."

"*The* Bobo Morgan!" Barry gasped.

"Well, if you don't believe me, come out to our farm this week end. Bobo'll be visiting us, and—"

She didn't need to say any more. We'd probably be waiting outside long before sunup

In the meantime we tried our best to get Sally to agree to being our regular coach for the rest of the summer ball season. We even offered her the tempting salary of one ice cream soda a week.

But Sally would have none of it.

"Oh, I'm not good enough to be a coach," she blushed modestly. "You see, baseball is just a sort of hobby with me."

It goes to show, you just never know, do you?

SQUEEZE PLAY

The ball got past Bob and the runner scooted for second

SQUEEZE PLAY

Catcher Bob Harkins squatted behind home plate. He glanced at the scoreboard down along the left field line.

Castle Junior High 7; Larchmont Junior High 4. It was the first half of the eighth inning. There was a Castle runner on second base. One out.

Bob stuck one finger down below his chest protector. It was the sign for a fast ball. Out on the mound, pitcher Vince Gordon shook off the signal. Bob tried again. He waggled his finger, the sign for a change of pace. Again the pitcher shook his head.

It had been going that way most of the game. Bob clenched his teeth. He knew the Castle batters better than Vince did. He knew their weaknesses. And, as catcher, it was his job to call the pitches. Yet Vince kept on refusing his signs.

"Time out, ump," Bob called. He pulled off his mask and strode out to the pitcher's mound.

Vince didn't even come in to meet him. He just stood there with his hands on his hips and let Bob walk the entire distance.

"Look, Vince," Bob tried to keep his voice calm. "How about agreeing with a few of the ones I call for? We've got to mix them up against these guys."

"How about you letting me pitch the

game?" Vince towered over him. "Your job is to catch them when they go past the batter."

"Not many have been going past," Bob said evenly. "Look at the scoreboard. Besides, you've been throwing way too many curves today. You know what Coach Sands says about young pitchers throwing a lot of curves. Not good for your arm."

"It's my arm," Vince insisted. "And if the coach wants, he can always take me out, can't he?"

It was the same old thing. And, as usual, Vince got in the last word. Bob turned and went back behind the plate.

The Castle batter stepped back into the box waggling his bat. "What is this, a brother act or something?" he asked with a smile.

Bob felt like saying "I wish it was," but he put on his mask without a word.

Vince checked the runner on second, then pitched. The ball started to curve toward the outside corner of the plate. But not many thirteen year old boys can throw a sharp breaking curve. Although Vince insisted that he was a curve ball artist, his pitches lacked plenty when it came to hooking in where he wanted them to. Now, instead of curving over the outside corner, the ball sailed in across the middle of the plate.

It was made to order for the Castle batter. Bob could even hear his grunt of satisfaction as he lashed into the pitch. The hard-hit ball sailed far out between right and center fields. The runner scored easily from second. The batter pulled up grinning on third.

Bob felt like asking Coach Sands to let someone else catch. What was the point in being a catcher if your pitcher didn't have any confidence in the way you called them? Bob knew that if he told the coach how Vince kept ignoring his signs, the tall pitcher would get a bawling out. Coach Sands was a strong believer in the catcher's being a sort of field general while the team was on the diamond. The catcher had the best chances to know the batters and to see that the rest of the team moved over to the general areas where each batter usually hit.

Yet, Bob knew that complaining to Coach Sands wasn't the right solution. The troubles between him and Vince had been going on for nearly a year. They were troubles that Bob knew would have to be worked out between them . . . if at all.

Vince kept shaking off about two out of every three signs that Bob gave him. Castle kept hitting. The score was 10 to 4 by the time the first half of the eighth inning was finished.

On the bench, shortstop Roddy Carter leaned over toward the catcher. "I'm not blind, Bob," he said. "I can read your pitching signs from shortstop. And, boy, I can sure see that Vince turns them down one after another. What's the matter with you two. For a brother team, you guys get along like cats and dogs. How come, Bob?"

"I . . . I guess Vince knows what he

wants," Bob said evasively. "He can pitch."

"Maybe so," Roddy agreed. "But it's sure not helping the score any."

"Quit worrying," Bob said stubbornly. "It will work out."

"I hope so, guy," Roddy said. "And it better be pretty soon. We're sure going to be in a big hole if we lose many more games."

Bob didn't think that any answer was necessary to that. But the problem between him and Vince was a personal one. And it wasn't all tied up with playing baseball, either.

He and Vince were brothers . . . at least, they were foster brothers, which shouldn't have made a bit of difference. Bob had lost his father in an accident several years ago. Then, last August, his mother had married Mr. Gordon. Bob not only had a new father, but a new brother as well.

But right from the start he and Vince hadn't gotten along. Although they were within six months of being the same age, they were just about as opposite temperamentally

104

as two boys could be. Bob was short, light-haired and freckle-faced. He worked hard for everything he got. On the other hand, Vince, tall and confident in everything he did, took all things in their stride. And Vince was good. There was no doubting that.

Ever since he had entered Larchmont Junior High, Vince had been a great help to the teams. He was a natural athlete. He had been a big star in football and basketball, although neither team had won the championship. They might have won at least one of the pennants if things had been a little different. One day toward the end of the football season, Coach Sands had called Bob aside. "You know," he said, "you and Vince are two of my best boys. You could make a great combination on any team . . . if you would just pull together."

"I know, coach. I know," Bob had admitted. That was about all there was to say. There was no point in making excuses. Sure, it was tough on the team to have a couple of players who sometimes seemed to be playing entirely different games. But Bob wondered if Coach Sands could guess what it was like at home. He wondered if the coach could guess what it would be like to live in the same house with your foster brother, and month after month remain strangers?

And during the past months things hadn't improved one bit.

Larchmont scored one run in the last half of the eighth inning. With Vince still insisting on throwing more curves than he should, Castle scored two runs of their own in the top of the ninth. The game soon ended.

Castle 12, Larchmont 5. It was Larchmont's worst defeat so far that season.

As usual, Bob and Vince left the locker room at different times. When Bob arrived home, Vince was already in his own room, off by himself. Even though they lived under the same roof, it was surprising how seldom the two boys saw each other. Bob never bothered Vince in his room, and the taller boy had never once gone out to the garage to accept Bob's invitation to play with his model train layout.

But when it came to mealtime, there was no avoiding each other. Usually either their mother or father would attempt to get an interesting conversation started. But more often than not it sort of faded away to nothing, as Bob and Vince kept their eyes on their plates. Bob knew that it worried both his mother and his new father. In fact, one day his mother had spoken to him about it.

"You two certainly are acting like small children," she scolded. "How did this dislike between you ever get started, anyway?"

But Bob hadn't been sure just what it was. He supposed you could call it just getting off on the wrong foot to start with. Ever since the first day that they had moved into the same house together, things had gone wrong between him and Vince. That first day Bob had raced around the corner of the house to greet his new brother. He had crashed blindly into him, knocking the taller boy to the ground and giving him a bloody nose. Of course, it had been an accident. But Vince had been pretty sore about it. It was a very bad start for a friendship.

It had grown worse after school began and they had found themselves competing for positions on the same teams. However, in both football and basketball Vince had been the one to come out ahead.

Somehow, almost everything that happened seemed to make their chances of getting along together that much slimmer. And each boy was just stubborn enough not to give in to the other.

Again today another game had been lost largely because they hadn't worked together in the close harmony that catcher and pitcher should.

The following Friday afternoon Larchmont played Medford. From the very beginning Vince insisted on pitching curves. Not every ball was a curve, but there were a lot more than there should have been. As usual, Vince shook off most of Bob's signs, and pitched exactly the way he felt like doing. For a while it worked pretty well. By the sixth inning Larchmont was ahead 6 runs to 4. But Bob could see that Vince was tiring. It was no easy job to keep throwing curves. They took a lot of extra effort. And now the Medford batters were getting on to them. In the last half of the sixth they got four hits, scored two runs and tied up the ballgame.

Bob didn't like to bring their arguments out in front of the other fellows. So he waited until Vince walked over to the water fountain, and then he followed.

"Vince," he said, "you've been doing swell. But your curve is slowing down now. They're onto it. How about letting me help out a little now? I've played against these guys several times. I know what they don't like. If you'll let me call them, I think we can fool the batters."

"Aren't you the great little guy, though?"

Vince said. "Just let you call them, and then you can tell everybody how you won the game."

"I didn't even have any such idea, Vince," Bob said quickly.

His foster-brother mopped the sweat from his forehead. "I don't need any help, pal. You just catch. I'll have these guys eating out of my hand."

Bob started to say something; then just shrugged and walked away. If there had been someone else who could catch behind the plate, he would have quit the game right then. This trouble between him and Vince had gone too far already. He was sick of it, and it certainly wasn't doing the team any good.

But there wasn't another catcher on the squad, any more than there was another pitcher as good as Vince. So, when Larchmont's turn at bat was finished, Bob picked up his mask and mitt and went back to his position.

The first Medford batter was their tall, loose-jointed left fielder. Bob remembered from other games that he was a sucker for low inside pitches. Bob held down one finger . . . the sign for a fast ball. Then he lifted his mitt as the target for Vince to aim at. But the pitcher shook his head, and waited for Bob to give him another sign. Nor did Vince nod agreement until Bob had exhausted the other possibilities and had finally given the sign for a curve.

It came in letter high with scarcely any break to it. The batter slammed it sharply back toward the pitcher's mound. Vince started to jump out of the way. Then he changed his mind and jabbed down with his bare hand. The speeding ball glanced off his hand and rolled across the diamond toward shortstop. Before Roddy Carter could get it, the runner was safe on first.

But Bob wasn't paying any attention to the runner. He had seen the sudden expression of pain that had crossed Vince's face the moment after he had tried to catch that ball with his bare pitching hand.

Now, as the ball was tossed back to him, Vince's face had a grim white look. It almost seemed to Bob that the tall boy was trying to hide something.

Bob called for a slow ball, but Vince again insisted on throwing a curve. The pitch was wild . . . into the dirt. It got past Bob, and the Medford runner scooted to second.

Bob looked up and saw that Vince's face still appeared sort of drawn.

"Time out, ump," he said, and walked out to the pitching mound.

Vince waited. But now there was no impatient hardness in his expression.

"Vince," Bob said, "what's the matter? Did . . . did you hurt your hand trying to catch that ball?"

The taller boy looked at him, and for a moment Bob thought that Vince was going to tell him to mind his own business or something. Then the pitcher glanced toward the ground.

"Yeah," he said softly, "I did. A little. Nothing bad. Just sort of bruised a finger, I guess, and—"

"Look," Bob cut in, "we better get someone else to pitch, don't you think?"

"Who?"

That, of course, was the big question. Larchmont was just a small junior high. They didn't have a whole string of reserve pitchers like some of the big schools. When you got

113

right down to it, Vince was the only one who could do any better than just lob the ball over the plate.

"Maybe you could trade off with Manny in right field," Bob suggested. "He used to pitch a little."

It seemed that Vince was giving it some thought. Manny wasn't much of a pitcher, but someone had to finish the game.

"I . . . I think I can stick in," Vince said.

"Not if you throw any more wild ones like that last one," Bob reminded. Yet he didn't want to press the subject of having Manny take the mound. This game with Medford was an important one. With three innings still left to play and the score tied, they wouldn't stand much of a chance of winning it with Manny on the mound.

"I . . . I guess I shouldn't have thrown that last curve," Vince admitted slowly.

"Sure," Bob bit out, "and you shouldn't have thrown a bunch of the others, either. So what?"

"So . . . well, maybe I could quit throwing curves," Vince looked at him levelly. "That last one rolled off my sore finger. That's why it went wild. But I'm sure I can throw a straight ball or a change of pace without it hurting much."

Bob didn't say anything for a moment. It wasn't easy to sympathize with a fellow who hadn't been trusting your judgment at all. Then Bob couldn't keep from saying, "That's what I've been trying to get you to do all along, fellow."

Vince scowled darkly. Then he smiled, "You still want to try it?" he said simply. "Or don't you? We need this game, you know."

Bob had the feeling that Vince wanted to say more, but just couldn't seem to bring himself to it. Overcoming stubbornness was not easy for either of them.

"Hey, boys," the umpire called. "Let's get the game going again."

"I'm willing to try it your way," Vince said again. There was almost a plea in his eyes. For the first time Bob realized just how much the game meant to the big pitcher. Maybe he had been wrong. Maybe Vince was more of a team player than Bob had thought.

But having been the underdog of the two for so long a time, the stocky catcher found it hard to be nice about it now. Besides, if Vince hadn't insisted on pitching those last two curves, the whole team probably wouldn't be in the present tough spot. Sure, with a bruised finger, Vince needed a catcher now. He needed a catcher who could tell him how and where to pitch the balls, and give him a good target. With Vince's curve ruined, it was their only chance of keeping the Medford batters from slamming the ball all over the diamond.

Now it was Vince who was doing the asking. Bob was tempted to let the pitcher get out of it any way he could. The big guy had been asking for this all season.

"You're the boss," Vince seemed puzzled by Bob's long silence. "What do you say? Should I let Manny finish up?"

Bob shook away the confusing thoughts that had been cluttering up his mind. This was no time to be holding onto a grudge.

"Let's you and me try it, Vince," he said.

"We can do it, Bob," Vince smiled broadly. "I know we can."

"One thing, though, Vince," Bob said. "If your finger gets any sorer will you promise to let me know?"

"Sure, Bob," the tall pitcher agreed. "But it won't. It's just a bruise. Feeling better already."

Bob felt better himself as he walked back toward the batter's box. Maybe at long last he and Vince had a common problem to solve. Thus far it had seemed that their biggest problem was each other.

But the game wasn't so easily won. Even though Vince's finger wasn't hurt badly, it was enough to spoil some of his control. One thing, though, he didn't shake off Bob's signs now. And he tried his best to lay them right into Bob's mitt. Some hit the target, some didn't. It was usually the ones that didn't that were knocked for fair hits. By the end of the seventh inning Medford led 8 runs to 6. Vince looked downcast.

"I'm trying, Bob," he said. "They just won't behave. Maybe I should have spent more time practicing control . . . instead of figuring on my curves."

"You're doing O.K., pal," Bob smiled. "Hey, Roddy," he called to the shortstop who was just stepping to the plate. "Start a rally. Let's get some hits. Paste that apple!"

It had been a long time since the little catcher had been in such good spirits. And the rest of the team seemed to sense the change. Whatever it was, they liked it. They took their turns at bat with a new determination. And they got results. Going into the last of the eighth inning, the score was again tied . . . 8-all.

Vince and Bob went back to the diamond. Vince's fast ball didn't have as much speed as usual, and his change of pace came in sort of tempting over the plate. But Vince was striving hard to put them right where Bob asked. Although he failed to fan any of the Medford batters, their hits turned into pop flies or easy grounders which the infield had little trouble in handling.

"Boy, Bob," Vince beamed, as Larchmont came in for its last turn at bat. "You sure know where those guys can't hit 'em. Sorry I can't get more of them right in there where you ask."

"You're doing O.K.," Bob said. "How's the finger?"

"Never felt better," Vince answered. But the finger was slightly swollen, making it seem that Vince might be doing a little fibbing.

Bob led off the inning with a sharp single through shortstop. Vince came up and dropped a bunt in front of the plate to sacrifice him to second.

With one away, outfielder Manny Proctor slammed a line drive over the first baseman's head. Bob romped home on the single. The next batter hit into a double play to retire the side.

But the score was Larchmont 9, Medford 8.

"Now," Bob said, snapping on his shin guards, "if we can just hold those monkeys for three more outs."

"We can do it, Bob," Vince was standing beside him. "You just call 'em where you want me to put 'em."

Try as he did, though, Vince walked the first batter.

"Think nothing of it, pal," Bob called to

him. "Just lay 'em in here, Vince." It was a plenty tough time to have a man on base. Last inning. No outs. And Larchmont leading by only one run. Vince looked plenty worried as he scuffed his toe in the dirt.

Bob figured that the next batter would try to sacrifice the runner to second so he would be in easy scoring position. That meant a bunt. He signalled to Vince for a high inside pitch. The boy on the mound nodded agreement, and Bob could even see the flicker of a knowing smile on the pitcher's face.

The pitch came in high and true. Vince came in halfway with it. Their guess had been right. The bunter wasn't able to pull the ball down on the ground. And Vince was right there to take it on the fly for the first out. He whirled quickly and pegged to first. It caught the surprised runner before he could get back to the base.

"Wow!" Bob ran out and pounded Vince gleefully on the shoulder. "That was one sweet play, brother!"

Vince turned and looked at him. "Just how do you mean that 'brother,' Bob?"

Bob hadn't really thought at the time he said it that the remark could be taken two ways.

"How would you like it to be meant?" he said, scarcely daring to smile.

"Well, we are brothers, aren't we?" Vince grinned. "We've got the same family."

"That's sure the way I'd like it, Vince," Bob said.

"That's the way I'd like it, too."

"Hey, you guys," the first baseman called. "Break up the party. The game isn't over yet. We've got one more put out to make."

Vince laughed. "I guess we better make him happy, huh, Bob?"

"Might as well," Bob grinned back. "Besides, let's get it over with and go home."

"Yeah," Vince said, "we've got lots of things to make up for, haven't we? I'd sure like to see that train setup you've got out in the garage."

Then they turned and started back to their positions. But anyone watching could tell that the two brothers weren't worried a bit about that last batter they still had to put out.

As a matter of fact, the two boys didn't seem to be worried about anything . . . not any more!

DIAMOND DOUBLE TROUBLE

The center fielder took one startled glance

DIAMOND DOUBLE TROUBLE

Ned Cooper stood up to the flat rock that was home plate. The bat was heavy on his shoulder.

"Come on, Ned," Ruth, his sister called from the sideline. "Give us a home run."

Someone laughed. Ned gulped, and tried to look as though he was right at home in the batter's box. But he was afraid that he wasn't fooling anyone, especially himself.

"Let him hit it, Cal," the Oak Knoll first baseman called to the pitcher. "Ned couldn't hit one out of the infield if you gave it to him on a platter."

"Yeah, come on in closer," the Oak Knoll catcher motioned to the Tiger infielders and outfielders both. Everyone moved in.

All of this ceremony made Ned wish he had stayed home. What were they trying to do . . . be smart alecks or something? But Ned had to admit that, according to his recent feats at bat, coming in close was the only wise thing for them to do. His hitting had been pretty terrible.

A quick glance at the scoreboard showed that the Oak Knoll Tigers were leading the Sage Center Cubs by one lone run . . . 7 to 6. The Cubs had runners on first and third. Two outs.

Ned tightened his grip on the bat. If he could just get a hit!

The first pitch came in low and outside. Ned let it go. The next one came in right over the center . . . big as a shoe store balloon. Ned took a mighty cut at it. Instead of the sharp click of bat against horsehide, there was a sort of dull thud. The ball dribbled down towards the Tiger shortstop. He trotted in to meet it, scooped it up and tossed easily to first base.

"What did I tell you," the Tiger first sacker laughed. "Ned swings that bat like it was a lead fencepost. Why don't you try swinging something lighter, guy," he jeered. "Something like the stick out of an all-day sucker?"

That brought a lot of laughs. Hot words rose into Ned's throat.

"Don't let them bother you, Ned," Ruth said as she passed by on her way out to left field. The Cubs being short of players, since Saturday was a pretty heavy chore day in the farming community, were using Ruth in the outfield. "Next time you'll sock that ball clear out of the pasture."

Ned twisted his lips into a half-smile. It was about the best he could do. He only wished he felt half as confident as Ruth sounded. He had let the Cubs down too often when a hit would have meant so much. The eyes of his teammates had lost a good deal of their friendliness toward him.

The first Tiger hitter cracked a grass cutter to the left of third base. Ned sprinted over, gobbled it up in his glove and rifled the throw to first. One away.

The next batter poled a long fly out to left field. Ruth raced back and to her right. The ball arched downward. She waited under it. The white pellet disappeared in her fielder's glove, but immediately appeared again rolling across the ground.

"Yipes!" Bobby Baxter moaned, "There she goes bobbling another one. We've got to locate a fellow to play out there. That's all there is to it."

130

The Tiger hitter pulled up grinning on second base. A minute later he scored on another outfield fly that Ruth dropped.

The game soon ended. The Oak Knoll Tigers headed across the fields toward home with a comfortable 9 to 6 victory under their belts.

Ned and Ruth walked along the rutted road toward their own home. Neither said much. After all, there wasn't much to say.

What had happened today was merely history repeating itself. Once again, the combination of Ned's poor hitting and Ruth's slippery-fingered catching had really lost the game for the Sage Center Cubs.

"I'm going to practice and practice," Ned blurted with sudden determination. "When we play those guys next week, I'll knock that ball into the next county."

"Sure you will," Ruth encouraged. But she was really worried about her own butter-fingers. "I . . . I kind of wish there were more boys living around here," she said. "Girls don't make very good ball players."

"Oh, you're going to show them yet, Ruth," Ned said. "Maybe we can practice together some. You catching and me hitting. If we don't beat the Tigers next week there'll be no living in the same valley with them."

But what Ned was really thinking was that unless things changed pretty quick, he and Ruth would be about as welcome on the Cub team as sandburrs in an alfalfa patch.

But the following day their plan to practice and improve their playing was given a serious setback.

"Oh, Ned," his father called, just as he was heading out behind the barn with ball and bat, "we've got to get that alfalfa on the north-forty loaded and under cover today. Some of it's getting pretty dry and bleached out."

Almost always before Ned had been able to get out of pitching hay, one way or another. But there was something about his father's tone of voice this morning that seemed to discourage making excuses.

Mumbling under his breath about never being able to hit the ball without getting in some practice, Ned laid down his bat and ball and headed for the barn to get a pitchfork.

Standing wide-legged on the bouncing bed of the wagon, Ned guided the team through the farmyard. He saw Ruth outside of the cookhouse. Evidently she had been drafted for work, too. She was fairly surrounded by wire baskets filled with eggs. She was helping

133

their mother candle them and put them in large crocks filled with a jelly-like stuff called waterglass. Thus preserved, the eggs would carry them through the fall and winter months when the chickens weren't laying much.

Things suddenly seemed to have taken a strange turn on the Cooper farm, Ned thought. Oh, he and Ruth had handled the small chores around the farm, but never before . . . well, pitching hay and preserving eggs were sort of grown-up-size jobs.

Nor was Ned so very happy over the sudden change. Maybe you couldn't call playing baseball more important than helping around home, but, well, it would be a pretty sad state of affairs if the Oak Knoll Tigers beat them again next Saturday.

And they surely would if he and Ruth didn't get in enough practicing to rid themselves of their batting and catching troubles.

It was nearly dark before the horses were unharnessed and fed. Ned was much too tired even to think of practicing his hitting. When he reached the house, Ruth was just washing the waterglass from her hands. She looked pretty tired, too.

"Well, sis," Ned said later, just before going to bed. "Maybe we can get in some practice tomorrow."

But the next day was the same. And the next. Ned had never realized that so much alfalfa hay could grow on a single forty-acre plot. By the end of the day he was sure that he had pitched at least three-quarters of all the hay in the world. His arms and shoulders and whole body ached.

"You're doing a good job, Ned," his father complimented that evening. "How does it feel to be doing a man's job?"

"Pretty good, Dad," Ned said without much enthusiasm. Secretly, he wished he was still just doing the boy-sized jobs like feeding the livestock, cleaning the chicken runs and stuff. Then he'd have time to practice batting.

Ruth was of much the same opinion. Handling and preserving eggs seemed to be a pretty responsible job for anyone her age . . . besides taking a lot of valuable time away from ball practice.

Fortunately, by Saturday the hay was all stacked in the barn loft, and the crocks filled with the preserved eggs were lined up in the cellar.

But as Ned and Ruth headed off across the fields toward the ball diamond, they were about as cheerful as two ducks in the middle of a desert.

"If only we could have put in some practice," Ned moaned. "Those Tigers are usually just a couple of hits better than we are. If I could just start pasting that ball."

"If I miss any more easy flies today," Ruth said, "I won't be able to look any of the team in the eye."

When they arrived at the diamond Bobby Baxter said, "Well, I guess you two will have to take your usual positions." He said it with a certain air of resignation that turned both Ned's and Ruth's cheeks apple-red.

For a moment Ned toyed with the idea of just going back home. Was it his fault that he couldn't get more power into his swings? They didn't have to rub it in! But he decided to stick it out. He didn't want to be called a quitter.

The Tigers went to bat first. Their previous victories made them confident.

"Let's finish this one up fast," Cal, their pitcher shouted. "It's a shame how easy it's going to be."

They all laughed . . . all the Oak Knoll Tigers, that is.

By the last of the third inning the score was Tigers 3, Cubs 0. Ned stepped to the plate for his first turn at bat. Bobby Baxter was on second base. One out.

"Jeepers," someone said behind him, just loud enough to reach Ned's ears. "It would have to be that guy's turn at bat. Talk about hard luck."

"Come on in close," the Tiger shortstop shouted to the fielders. "Old rusty-swing is with us again."

Ned squeezed on the bat so tight that his hands ached. Then he forced himself to relax his grip.

The count climbed to two balls and two strikes. The next pitch came in chest high. Ned watched it closely, and swung.

Click! The sharp smack of horsehide against hickory echoed across the diamond. The center fielder took one startled glance over his head, then spun on his heel and started running back for all he was worth. Before he even caught up with the ball, Bobby had crossed home plate and Ned was close behind him.

"Accidents will happen," the Tiger first baseman tried to console his teammates, as the score keeper chalked up a big "2" for the Cubs.

But, for some strange reason, Ned felt that it hadn't been an accident.

And to prove it, he repeated the performance in the last of the sixth, bringing in two more runs.

Each team got one run in the eighth inning.

Cubs 5, Tigers 4. Now there were some worried faces on the Tiger team. Just as there were some mighty puzzled faces on the Cub nine.

The Oak Knoll Tigers went to bat for their last chance in the first of the ninth. And their best brace of batters was coming up.

"We've got to hold them," Bobby pleaded. "Just three more outs."

The one-run lead had to hold!

But things soon took a turn for the worse. The first Tiger smacked one over the second baseman's head for a single. Then the Cubs got mixed up on covering a bunt. By the time the dust cleared, Tiger runners were safe on first and second. The next two batters were put out, but the runners had moved to second and third. A hit now would practically mean the game for the Tigers.

Ned felt awful. After his two swell hits, which had brought in four of the Cubs' five runs, now they stood a good chance of losing the lead.

And to make it even worse, the Tigers' strongest batter strode up to the plate. He took a good cut at the first pitch.

Crack! The ball soared skyward. The runners dug out for home plate. Every player on the Sage Center team was ready to call it quits. This was too much! For the ball was going far and high into left field. Toward Ruth . . . who hadn't caught a fly like that in a blue moon.

But Ruth hadn't given up. She was streaking across the field after that long fly ball. Her feet churned beneath her over the uneven ground.

At the last moment, while she was still running at full speed, her hand stretched out over her head. The ball disappeared.

Everyone waited breathlessly . . . waited to see the ball bounce out and go rolling off across the ground as it usually did.

But the ball didn't appear again, until

Ruth stopped, picked it out of her glove and held it high for everyone to see.

And that was the game! Sage Center Cubs 5, Oak Knoll Tigers 4.

For a few moments everyone just stood stunned. They just couldn't seem to believe what their own eyes had seen. Then everyone on the Cub team began to yell and shout.

It was quite a while before Ned and Ruth

could break away from their happy team-mates.

"Ned, you were just as great as they all said," Ruth confirmed as they headed across the fields toward home. "You handled that bat as though . . . well, almost as though it was a feather. And it always used to seem so heavy the way you tried to swing it."

"Well, it was much lighter today," Ned said. "But then maybe it only seemed so, after pitching those heavy forkfuls of hay all week. Just look at these muscles." And he flexed his arms playfully. Then, suddenly a strange light came into his eyes, as though he had just realized what he had said. "Ruth! That's it! Helping Dad . . . hey, who'd ever believe that you could actually be helping yourself to play better ball by . . . by doing things like pitching hay? Boy, I better not tell Dad!"

Ruth suddenly stopped, as though she had just been stricken by a thought of her own.

"Ned, those fly balls I caught today," she said. "Usually I dropped them. But today

. . . well, you don't suppose that handling those eggs all week . . . that maybe it cured me of being a butterfingers."

They looked at each other, but neither said a word.

They were much too happy to go delving into deep problems like that.

TUBBY TURNS
THE TRICK

"That's no beach ball. That's Tubby!"

TUBBY TURNS
THE TRICK

It was mostly loyalty on Tubby Melton's part. The note on the bulletin board had said that more players were needed to fill out the eighth grade baseball team. Tubby was an eighth grader. He was loyal to his class.

And although he didn't consider himself a very good ball player, he could certainly fill out almost anything.

Now, as he looked into the large mirror on the wall of the boy's locker room, he wondered just how far his loyalty should go. The image that stared back at him was definitely on the plump side. It had a shock of straw-colored hair that seemed to explode in all directions. Right under it was a round cheerful face all splattered with hundreds of freckles. A stubby nose perched between two eager green eyes. The rest of him was like—well, looking at the image in the mirror, he didn't wonder why everyone called him Tubby.

"Oh, no," he said to the reflection in the mirror. "Can that be a ball player?"

Then he struck a pose. "Well, I may not look like Ralph Kiner or Joe DiMaggio," he said. "But Tubby will do his best for the eighth grade and Redlands Junior High."

He squared his shoulders, tilted his cap at a saucy angle and strode out to the diamond.

148

"Hey, look," some one shouted. "One of you guys roll that beach ball off the field!" It sounded like Del Harper's voice.

"Sure," another laughed. "I'll kick it . . . hey, that's no beach ball. That's Tubby!"

Everyone laughed then. Even Tubby couldn't hold back a grin. He was used to it, and he really didn't mind. His fatness was his one big claim to fame around Redlands Junior High. The fellows had never been able to get him down with their kidding. There was never anything cruel in it, anyway.

Del Harper was the only one who ever got under Tubby's skin. But, then, the big pitcher would razz anyone who wasn't as good as he. And few of the fellows at Redlands were. Del was tall, dark-haired, husky and always sure of himself. He walked over to the short, stout boy, pounding the ball in his glove with the air of a big league player.

"You've played baseball before, haven't you, Tubby?" he asked. "I'm pitcher and captain. It's my job to know how good you are."

149

"Oh, I've caught a few balls in my time," Tubby said grandly.

"What's your batting average?" Del asked.

"Boy, oh, boy," Chuck Gail broke in. "Listen to Del. Hey, captain, save your speeches for next Wednesday's assembly. Tubby's no dunce. He knows how to play ball. Else he wouldn't be out here, would he?"

"All right, boys," Coach Meadows called, as he walked across the diamond toward them. "Take your places on the field. Tubby, just what is your favorite position?"

"Tubby would make a good backstop," one of the players said, "No ball could get past him."

"I'm no catcher, coach," Tubby objected. "Anything else, maybe."

"How about right field, then?"

"Sure," Tubby agreed, and trotted his roly-poly figure out beyond first base.

He had hardly reached his position when the sound of a hard hit ball spun him around. He saw it arching toward him, and ambled after it as fast as his stubby little legs would move. He speared out a hand to stop it.

"Ouch!" he yelped, as the ball hit his outstretched hand. "That thing's hard as a rock."

"How can you tell?" Del called out. "You're plenty padded. And go after those a little faster. You've got a lot of field to cover."

"Tubby's just the one who can cover it," someone laughed.

"If you guys would quit trying to be so funny," Chuck scolded, "maybe we could get some practicing done."

As practice went on, Tubby chased balls until he was ready to drop. Yet, he kept plodding after each one for all he was worth.

"That's the spirit, chum," Chuck called.

"Sure, but spirits don't catch balls," Del yelled. "If Tubby would catch some of those when they're coming to him, instead of chasing them after they've gone past, it might help. Maybe he'd even be some good to the team some day."

Tubby swallowed hard. "Maybe even before you, huh, Del?" he challenged. He didn't usually argue with his classmate. But he was getting tired of Del's picking on him.

At bat, Tubby let a low ball go by without taking the bat off his shoulder.

"Nice eye, Tubby," Chuck grinned.

"Sure," Del scoffed, "nice eye. But try using both of them and maybe you can get a hit."

Maybe the eighth grade captain meant it all in good fun. It was the strange kind of fun that Del seemed to glory in. His razzing was fairly harmless, and Tubby could usually shake it off without a second thought.

But now it began to cut deeply. Especially when he was doing all he could to be of some use to the team.

It was during the game with Eastview Junior High's eighth grade team that Tubby made his first costly error. Not that he hadn't made quite a few before. But they were during practice, and hadn't really counted.

The score was 7 to 5 in favor of Redlands.

152

It was the last half of the final inning. There were two Eastview runners on base. Two outs.

It was a tense moment. When a left-handed batter stepped to the plate, Chuck turned and called back to Tubby. "Watch out, guy. This batter usually pulls his hits into right field."

Tubby nodded and leaned slightly forward so that he would be ready to go in any direction at the crack of the bat. But if there was anything that the portly outfielder hoped wouldn't happen, it was to have that ball come out his way. He hadn't been so very good with his catches, even during practice. And now, with the tieing run on base and the winning run at bat, he just hoped that ball would choose some other direction.

The batter swung at the very first pitch. The solid crack of the bat on the ball signalled a hard hit. As soon as he saw the white ball rising against the blue sky Tubby knew that it was heading right for him. A sudden chill surged along his spine.

Tubby watched the ball reach its peak and

start down. He raised his glove and waited. Then, suddenly, he couldn't see it in the white glare of the sun. A wave of panic swept over the stubby right fielder. The ball completely missed his glove, and a loud groan went up from the rooters.

Tubby turned and chased after the ball. But by the time he got to it and made his throw, all three Eastview runners had crossed home plate. Eastview had won, 8 to 7.

Gloom hung heavy in the locker room. Everyone seemed too disappointed or too angry to say anything. Chuck was the first to speak up. "What . . . what happened, Tubby? That didn't look like a very tough ball to catch out there."

But Tubby had never liked the idea of making excuses. He just shrugged and finished tying his shoelaces.

"Sun in his eyes, I suppose," Del said with sarcasm. "That's as good an excuse as any."

Although Del had hit the nail on the head, Tubby still held his silence. But he knew one

154

thing. He was going to get some sun glasses. That is, if he still got to play in right field after the costly error he had made.

"Well, let's forget the game," Chuck suggested. "There'll be others."

And there were others . . . Marysville, Lincoln, Piedmont, South and Canfield. The

Redlands eighth graders won their share of the victories. But a rather skimpy share, at that. Which meant that if they didn't start doing better, they couldn't hope to be the eighth grade champions of the city schools.

Tubby played each game with a certain dread. It was caused by that first game with Eastview. It was the dread of missing another fly ball that might cost Redlands another game. It seemed that nearly every right field in the league faced directly into the sun.

Yet, with each game, the stocky right fielder felt that he was improving. In fact, Chuck Gail was even kind enough to mention it after the Canfield game. "You're getting better, pal," he said. "A lot better. You missed only one fly out there today. I guess those sun glasses help, huh?"

"Oh, sure," Tubby agreed, "they help some." But, although he didn't tell Chuck, the glasses had a habit of not wanting to stay put on his stubby nose. They would slide down and the bright sun would come over the upper rim and glare right in his eyes.

That's what had happened today when he had missed that one fly ball.

Tubby was determined to solve the problem one way or another, though. He might make a few errors out there, but no one could ever accuse him of not trying.

All of the eighth graders were excited during the next week. Several of the top teams had been upset by some of the lesser teams. Coach Meadows showed them a paper with a bunch of figures on it. They all added up to the fact that whoever won Friday's game between Madison and Redlands would be the new champions of the eighth grade league.

"Boy, oh, boy," Chuck said. "Redlands hasn't won the eighth grade trophy for six years. This is our one big chance."

But as the big day approached for the game, there was a feeling of worry among the players. Del put the feeling into words.

"You guys have got to quit making errors out there," he said. "And, Tubby, that goes double for you."

"Yes sir, your highness," Tubby held onto

a grin. But he knew his face must be red. It didn't seem right that Del would single him out, when everyone had made errors.

Practically all of the Redlands students walked over to Madison Junior High on Friday afternoon to see the big game. The small grandstand along the first base line was one big splash of color that sparkled gaily in the bright afternoon sun.

Del paced back and forth along the side lines. He kept rubbing his hands together, then wiping them on his shirt.

"Hey, cap," Tubby said, "why don't you take it easy? You'll need all your strength when you go out there to pitch."

"Look, don't worry about me," the tall pitcher said sharply. "I can take care of the chucking, all right. The big worry is that no one out there in the field starts making a bunch of errors. Can't afford sloppy fielding in this game."

Tubby didn't need to be hit on the head. He knew pretty well just what field Del

158

meant. Of course, it was right field . . .
which meant Tubby.

The game soon started. Everyone knew
from the moment that the first Madison batter stepped to the plate in the last half of the
first inning that it was going to be a close and
hard-fought game. Del was unusually tense in
the pitcher's box. It was only through some
good playing by the infield that Madison
didn't score in the first inning.

The second inning also went scoreless for
both teams.

In the last of the third inning Tubby let a
fast grounder get through his legs. By the
time he had waddled after it and got off his
throw, the batter had gone all the way to third
base.

The next hit was a long fly ball into left
field. The runner tagged up, and scored easily
after the catch.

"I . . . I'm sorry I missed that ball,"
Tubby apologized as the inning finally ended.

"Don't tell me the sun was in your eyes

way down on the ground!" Del said flatly.

An answer rose to Tubby's lips, but he bit it back and found a place on the bench. He

thought of the practicing he and his father had been doing at home.

Redlands scored two runs in their half of

the fifth inning, to go out ahead. But in the last of the sixth, Madison came back with another run to tie up the ball game at 2-all.

The seventh and eighth innings were scoreless.

Then, in the first of the ninth, Chuck hit a two-bagger with only one out. The next Redlands batter socked a long fly into right field. The Madison fielder who had declined Tubby's offer to lend him his dark glasses, was blinded by the sun. He dropped a long high fly and Chuck trotted in to score. The batter was thrown out, a moment after Chuck had crossed home plate, by trying to stretch a double into a triple.

Now, everyone on the Redlands team seemed more cheerful. That one run lead in the ninth inning might well be the winning run of the ball game.

"Boy, oh, boy!" Del crowed. "That's it! All I've got to do is hold them for three more outs and the championship is in the bag."

The next Redlands batter fanned out to

end the first half of the final inning. Redlands 3, Madison 2.

"Good luck, Del," Tubby said, as he hurried past the pitcher's mound on his way out to right field. "Game's practically won."

"Don't be counting your chickens," the team captain scowled. "And try to keep heads up out there. If you go dropping a ball now, I'll—"

"You just pitch, Del," Tubby cut in sharply. "You do your best—I'll do mine." He was surprised by his own stern words.

The first Madison batter lined a drive to the left of the pitcher's mound. The first baseman raced over fast and scooped up the horsehide. Del, like any good pitcher, should have rushed over to cover first base. But he didn't seem to think of it in time, and the runner sprinted across the bag safe. The crowd jeered the big pitcher's costly oversight.

"What's the matter with you, Del?" the first baseman complained. "How did you expect me to get that ball and also get back to first in time? You really butched that one good."

Del moved his lips in an apology, but no words came out. He knew that he had been asleep on the play. He also knew that, with no outs, the runner had a better than even chance of scoring before the inning was over. That would be enough to tie the game. A couple of hits would win it . . . for Madison.

Del stood on the pitcher's mound, fingering the ball nervously.

"It's O.K., boy," Tubby called from right field. "I should have been in there, too."

People along the sidelines laughed at the idea of the roly-poly Tubby being able to reach first base in time to catch that runner.

Even Del smiled. He seemed a little more relaxed because of it. That was reward enough for Tubby. If it helped the pitcher to settle down a little, Tubby didn't mind if the others laughed.

163

But Del wasn't nearly as relaxed as he tried to look. The next Madison batter knocked a long fly ball to deep left field. The Redlands fielder chased back after it and made a great catch over his shoulder.

But, having seen that hit, which had come mighty close to being a home run and losing the game for Redlands, Del looked limp and weak-kneed.

One out . . . the runner still on first base. It could be a lot worse, Tubby reasoned.

And it soon was.

Del's control seemed suddenly to have left him. He walked the next batter, putting runners on first and second.

Del rubbed dirt on his hands, squared back his shoulders and fired the next pitch over the catcher's head. The runners advanced to second and third.

Only one out. A hit now would win the ball game for Madison.

The big Redlands pitcher looked like a puppy that had just been whipped. Even from way out in right field, Tubby could see Del's hands tremble.

"Time out!" Chuck called to the umpire. "Hold everything!"

Tubby knew that it was a smart move on the second baseman's part. When everything started going against you, it was always a good time to pause, take a deep breath and try to figure out what was wrong. Most of the Redlands team crowded in around the big pitcher, trying to calm him down and give him back his confidence.

"Look," Chuck said, nodding toward the Madison batter who was waiting impatiently at the plate. "I've been watching that fellow. He likes them high and outside. Try to pitch him some low, inside ones. How about it, Del?"

At any other time, Del Harper probably would have argued that he knew what he was doing and for Chuck to play his own position. The tall pitcher was one guy who really disliked being told what to do. But now he just mopped at the sweat that beaded his forehead. "O.K.," he said without argument. "I'll do my best."

It struck Tubby as strange just how fast Del's boastful confidence had melted away. For once Del seemed to realize that there was a whole team behind him . . . pulling for him and backing him up on each play.

"Play ball!" the umpire called.

Del's first pitch was low and inside, just as Chuck had said. The batter swung feebly at it and missed.

But something went wrong with the next pitch. It went floating in toward the batter, high and outside . . . right where he liked them.

Bat cracked against horsehide. A loud groan arose from the Redlands rooters, as the ball started its long flight out into right field. Tubby saw it coming. He raced backwards, hoping that he wouldn't suddenly stumble.

Out of the corner of his eye, Tubby caught a glimpse of the Madison runner on second take a long lead off the base. That Madison player no doubt wanted to be well on his way to scoring the winning run in case Tubby dropped the fly. The runner on third was tagging up, figuring he could score whether the fly was caught or not.

Then as Tubby raised his gloved hand above his head to shield his eyes, the large thumb caught on his sun glasses and ripped them off. They fell to the ground. Tubby heard the crunch of glass under his heel. He stood horrified as the ball arched toward him, moving directly into the blinding light of the sun.

It was now or never, he thought. In the fleeting moment the ball fell toward him out of the glaring sky, Tubby remembered all of the practicing he had been doing at home, trying to be prepared for just such a moment as this one.

But now that it was really happening, it was all Tubby could do to keep from turning his back to the blinding glare of the sun and hope that the ball didn't hit him on the head.

He crowded back the urge. He held his

arms out, judging the ball's flight just as he had been practicing. He followed its flight until it began to disappear in a dazzling spray of white light. Then he waited.

It was only an instant, but it seemed a year before the ball struck. Tubby felt it hit the edge of his glove, and start to fall away. He grabbed desperately for it, and caught it just before the ball hit the ground.

During all of this, Tubby was remembering how the Madison runner had taken such a big lead off second base. As soon as he got the ball, the fattish right fielder whirled and threw with all of his might toward second. Chuck was standing with one foot planted on the bag. The Madison runner scurried back. But Tubby's throw was true to its mark. It beat the runner to the base by a step, ending the inning and the game.

Redlands Junior High 3, Madison Junior High 2.

Redlands was the new eighth grade champion of the city junior high school league!

Del was the first one to reach Tubby. He

was closely followed by Chuck and the others.

"Boy, you were sure lucky, Del," Chuck scolded. "You grooved that last pitch right where that batter wanted it. How come?"

"I . . . I couldn't help it, Chuck," Del swallowed. "It sort of slipped. Boy, oh, boy, Tubby, if it hadn't been for you! When you knocked off your glasses and I saw that sun shining right smack in your eyes, I thought—"

"None of us could have blamed you, Tubby," Chuck cut in. "Not even if you had missed that fly. No sir, not with the sun shining smack in your eyes."

"Well, it wasn't exactly in my eyes," Tubby smiled. "I finally read how big league players manage that sometimes. They've got a little trick. I practiced it a lot."

"What's the trick, Tubby?" Del asked. "It sure saved my skin. I'd like to know it, too."

"Oh, it's not much," Tubby said. "It's just that you don't watch the ball go right into the sun. You sort of look to one side, and you can still see it pretty good out of the corner of your eye without actually looking at it. Then you know just where it is when it comes out of the glare. Then you snag it . . . like I almost didn't do," Tubby laughed.

"And you practiced it that way?" Del asked.

"Sure, doesn't it take practice to learn most anything? My dad and I play catch after he gets home from work. I always practice facing the sun."

"Boy," Del said, "am I a sap. I just figured that you came out for the team because you didn't have anything else to do. How about you and me being friends, Tubby?"

Tubby looked around him. He felt a little embarrassed. But all the other fellows were grinning now. Several of them were pounding Tubby on the back and rumpling his hair.

Everyone was being might friendly. And if there was anything that Tubby really liked more than anything, it was friends.

"It's a deal!" he laughed, holding out his hand.

"A big deal!" the others chorused; then broke in a run toward the waiting school bus.

EVEN STEPHEN

"You did that on purpose, Butch," he accused

EVEN STEPHEN

The bright morning sun sprinkled through the leaves of the giant elms that bordered the streets of Daly City. The members of the Redwing team were full of horseplay, as they hiked along on their way to the public playground.

Shortstop Ziggy Pitts plucked a couple of wild sunflowers that were growing beside the walk. He sneaked up behind Milo Perry and dropped them into his catcher's mask.

173

"There's a bouquet for you, chum," Ziggy laughed.

"Aw, cut it out, will you," Milo said seriously. "Quit trying to be so funny."

Ziggy erased the smile from his face. Some of the others turned and looked at Milo. It wasn't at all like the peppery catcher to act like that. In fact, Milo was usually right in the middle of their fun.

"He's just worried about having to play against Butch Carson again," someone said.

"Maybe you can't blame him," first baseman Lefty Lewis added. "You can still see a little of that black eye Butch gave him the last time we played the Otters."

Milo winced slightly at the memory. And Lefty wasn't far from guessing right, either. The thought of having to play another game against Butch Carson didn't make Milo very happy.

The public playground league had been going along swell, as far as Milo was concerned, until Butch Carson had started play-

174

ing third base for the Otters. Butch had always been pretty much of the bully type, even at school. Like most such fellows, he had his favorites to pick on. Milo was one of them. But Milo was no sissy. During their last game with the Otters, Butch had tripped him as he went into third base. Of course, he had done it slyly so that the umpire didn't see it. Then, before Milo could scramble up, the grinning third baseman had tagged him out.

Milo didn't usually lose his temper. But that time he saw red. It hadn't been the first time Butch had pulled some such fancy trick. Milo got up and waded into the larger boy with his fists flying. The next thing he knew he was lying in the dirt, holding a hand over his eye, and Butch was standing over him, grinning.

Now, as he thought back on it, Milo wasn't very happy over the prospect of today's game with the Otters.

They soon arrived at the playground. The

Otters were already warming up on the diamond. They stopped and let the Redwings have their turn.

"Just give us the signal when you're ready," the Otter captain said.

"Yeah," Butch Carson called, "let us know when we can start the massacre."

Milo glanced over at the big third baseman. Butch had sort of reddish hair. He was dressed in a T shirt, blue jeans and tennis shoes, which was what most of the fellows wore during the summer playground league games. Butch was a little on the heavy side, but most of it was muscle. He had one front tooth missing. It gave Milo a slight feeling of pleasure to think that in one of the bully's many fights someone must have gotten in at least one good blow.

The players soon were ready to start the game. The Redwings went to bat first. Milo led off with a single. Lefty Lewis popped a fly to deep short for the first out. A minute later Milo raced to second on a wild pitch. With a two ball and two strike count, Brick

176

Hadley slammed a long fly into right field. Milo tagged up and waited for the catch. As soon as the ball was in the fielder's glove, he sprinted toward third base.

He could tell by the shouting that it was going to be a close race between him and the ball. But the third base coach didn't give him the sign to slide, so Milo raced in standing up. Butch Carson was straddling the base. Milo's foot hit the bag just before the ball plopped into the third baseman's glove.

But Butch didn't give up that easily. He shoved out his hip, knocking Milo off balance. Then, before the Redwing runner could get his foot back on the base, the burly Otter infielder tagged him hard.

"How about that, ump?" Butch pointed to Milo's foot.

"Your foot's off the base, son," the umpire called. "You're out!"

Once more Milo saw red. "You did that on purpose, Butch," he accused. "You shoved me off the bag!"

"Didn't you hear what the umpire said,

junior?" the third baseman snapped. "You're out. Quit arguing and play ball."

Well, Milo wasn't going to make the same mistake twice and pick a fight with Butch Carson. But, as he squatted behind home plate to begin the second half of the inning, Milo promised himself that he would get even with the cheating third baseman somehow.

Butch had anything but a soft voice. He started out right away to heckle the Redwing pitcher, Art Ryan. But on the mound Art was always as cool as a mountain brook. So Butch soon turned his attention to Milo.

"You couldn't catch flies with molasses," he yelped. "Watch out, watch out, watch out!"

Razzing by players of the other team was all a part of baseball. It didn't usually bother Milo. But Butch Carson seemed to go on and on without even taking a breath. Nor was there anything good humored or witty about his shouts.

178

The Redwing catcher gritted his teeth and tried to concentrate on Art Ryan's pitches. But the confusion that Butch was creating

seemed to have its effect. With one out on the Otters, Milo gave the sign for a fast inside pitch. Only after the batter had smacked it into center field for a double, did Milo remember numbly that he was just the batter who liked them fast and inside.

The next hitter grounded out to second base. But the base runner sprinted to third on the play. Two outs.

It was then that Butch Carson pulled his second stunt of the game. A slight breeze was blowing into Milo's face from the general direction of left field. Once in a while little eddies of flying dust would trickle along the ground toward him. Butch seemed to have noticed them, too. For, with the count one ball and two strikes against the batter and the Otter runner on third, Butch just seemed to be waiting his chance.

Then, just as a gust of wind came up, Butch scuffed his foot in the dirt along the base line. The wisp of wind picked up the brown cloud of dust and bore it down toward Milo just as Art Ryan cut loose with his fast ball.

The dust bit into Milo's eyes. He missed the pitch completely. The Otter runner scampered home to score the first run of the game.

Milo complained bitterly to the umpire.

But the umpire wasn't sure that Butch had done it purposely. Although he warned the innocent-looking third baseman against doing such a thing again, the run counted.

"We ought to quit playing these guys," Lefty Lewis complained a little later when the Redwings came in for their second turn at bat. "I saw that stunt Butch pulled on you, Milo."

"Don't worry," Milo said. "I'll get even with that guy. My chance will come. And, boy, he better watch out when it does."

Milo felt some of their eyes on him.

"You sound different, guy," Lefty said. "None of us has ever known you to play dirty or unfair. Better watch yourself, huh?"

It was a strange warning, Milo thought. No one ever before had cautioned him about being a good sport. They hadn't needed to. But there came a time, Milo figured, when you had to fight fire with fire.

At the end of four innings, the Otters were leading by one run, 4 to 3. Butch Carson seemed to have no intention of letting up on

Milo. He rode him hard all of the time. And, although Milo kept his eyes open for a chance, he never was able to get back on the big, blustery third baseman. Words certainly weren't enough. Milo didn't bother to waste them trying to razz Butch.

The game was scheduled for seven innings, according to their playground league rules.

Then, in the last half of the fifth inning, the Redwings began to get the range on the Otter pitcher's stuff. Ziggy Pitts, a left hand hitter, pulled an inside pitch along the first base line. The baseman managed to knock it down, but couldn't get hold of it in time to beat Ziggy to the bag.

"Nice single, Ziggy," Milo yelled. At the same time, he motioned for the next batter to lay down a bunt and sacrifice Ziggy to second. That would put the little shortstop in scoring position. Right now one run was mighty important. The score was still 4 to 3 in favor of the Otters.

The bunt worked. Art Ryan came to bat with one out and a runner on second. Art

182

was one fellow who didn't believe in the saying that you couldn't be a pitcher and a hitter both. He swung into the third pitch, and connected solidly. The ball sailed over Butch Carson's head into left field. Ziggy scored the tieing run. Art pulled up grinning with a double.

Redwings 4, Otters 4. One out.

Van Holt, the next batter, let the first three pitches go by. Two balls and one strike. The fourth one was right where he liked it. He pounded a line drive through the slot between first and second. The right fielder raced in after it. Art was rounding third and heading home with the tie-breaking run. But just as he rounded third, Butch Carson went through the motions of trying to get out of the base path. But his motions were slow, and Art had to swing out around the third baseman on his way to home plate. It cost him several precious steps.

In the meantime, the Otter right fielder had scooped up the ball and pegged it toward home. The catcher got it on the first bounce.

Although Art tried to slide in under the tag, the Otter catcher had the ball on him before his foot touched the plate.

Van had raced to second on the throw.

Milo jumped off the bench and faced the umpire. "Butch blocked the base path, ump!" he yelled. "Didn't you see how he stalled around before he got out of Art's way? That's illegal, ump. Art should be safe. Blocking. Butch blocked!"

But all of his yelling was to no avail. Art was called out, and Butch Carson, having trouble hiding a grin, had once again gotten away with one of his tricks.

The next batter flied out. The game was still tied at 4-all.

Art Ryan bore down for all he was worth in the first of the sixth inning. He fanned the first batter, and forced the second to pop a weak fly to shortstop. Then Milo snagged a high foul near the Otter bench for the final out of the inning.

"Come on, Milo," Lefty Lewis said, as the

184

Redwings came in to bat. "Start it out, pal. Let's break this tie."

"Hot dog," Butch Carson bellowed from third. "Here's an easy out! Serve it to him on a platter. He couldn't hit a cow if he was riding on its back."

Milo lashed into the second pitch. The ball skittered across the ground to Butch

185

Carson's left. The big infielder stabbed out his glove. But he bobbled the ball a moment. By the time he made his throw, Milo had reached first. Safe. Butch kicked viciously at the dirt.

A moment later Milo raced to second after Lefty's long fly into center field.

One out, and Milo with the tie-breaking run in scoring position.

Brick Hadley came to bat next. He let a called strike go by. Milo took a long lead off second, and flashed Brick the sign for a hit-and-run.

The next pitch was way low. But Brick swung at it, anyway, as he was supposed to do on the hit-and-run signal. He missed, but the Otter catcher had trouble trapping the ball in his mitt, and Milo scampered into third, safe.

Now was the big chance. One out. Any hit by Brick, other than a fly ball to the in-field, would score Milo. And Brick was a long-ball hitter.

186

Brick watched the next two pitches go by for called balls. Then he connected solidly with an outside curve. The ball arched into short right field. With only one out, Milo held his foot on third. He was certain that he could beat the right fielder's throw to home after the catch. He was sure he could score the big run . . . probably the winning run.

Then the ball was dropping down toward the fielder. The moment that it disappeared into his glove, Milo shoved off the base toward home plate.

But he hadn't noticed Butch standing right there on the base beside him, practically touching him. He hadn't noticed the strange pressure on his belt. Yet, when he broke toward home after the catch, he felt it. A quick tug. Just enough to hold him back for a moment!

But that moment was exactly the extra time needed for the right fielder's throw to beat him to home plate. Milo dove head-

187

first under the throw. But the Otter catcher jabbed the ball on him, while his hand was still groping for the rubber.

"Out!" the umpire jerked his thumb up over his shoulder.

Milo was too angry to speak. Tears welled up in his eyes as he brushed the dirt from his clothes. Butch Carson walked to the bench without even glancing his way. Milo knew that the big bullying third baseman must have a grin on his face. He also knew that no one had seen Butch hook his finger in Milo's belt and hold him back. If accused of such a thing, the unsportsmanlike third baseman would surely deny it. It had happened before. Milo knew that there was not much use in his squawking.

As he pulled on his shin guards and chest protector, Milo promised himself bitterly that he never again would play in a game with Butch Carson.

Milo tried to concentrate on the game there in the first half of the seventh and final inning. But his thoughts kept going back to all of the dirty tricks Butch had pulled that afternoon . . . and other afternoons. The short catcher felt horribly robbed that he hadn't had a single chance to get even with the third baseman.

Milo was scarcely aware of what was taking place until Art Ryan called a time-out and came striding in off the pitcher's mound.

"What's the matter with you, pal?" Art said. "Are you dreaming back here? You've been giving me the signs for just the wrong pitches to these guys."

"Jeepers," Milo sort of shook himself mentally. "I . . . I'm sorry, Art. I . . . I guess I wasn't thinking—"

"Well, start thinking now," Art scolded. "If we let that runner on third get in, we're sunk. With two outs, all we have to do is fan that big moose out, and—"

"Moose?" Milo said absently.

"Butch."

"Butch!"

"Are you sick, Milo?" Art looked alarmed.

"Me? No," Milo said. "I'm O.K. Come on. We'll get Butch!"

Art shook his head and went back to the mound. Butch Carson came up to the plate, waving his bat and grinning.

"Just throw it and jump out of the way," he yelled.

Now Milo's thoughts came back to the game. He glared at the figure hovering over the plate. He gave Art the sign for a fast, inside pitch.

The ball came in true. Butch swung and missed. Milo grinned behind his mask.

"There you are, big boy," he taunted. "And watch out for another one just like—"

Suddenly he stopped. For, while he was talking, he noticed the bat that Butch was using. And he noticed something about the bat that made the hair on his scalp sort of tingle.

There was a crack . . . a thin, hair-like

190

crack, but a deep one . . . right above where Butch gripped the handle firmly.

Right where it was almost sure to snap if the big third baseman hit the ball!

At first sight of it, a sort of grim smile crossed Milo's face. Butch would never be able to hit a ball out of the infield with that bat! And an infield hit now, with the Redwings playing in close, was almost sure to be an out. It would end the Otter's scoring threat. With strong Redwing hitters coming up in the last of the seventh, they were almost sure to win the game.

Milo started to give his next signal to Art, who was watching puzzled from the mound.

This, Milo thought grimly, was his big chance to get even with Butch Carson! This was what he had been waiting for!

But, even as those thoughts raced through his mind, he felt sort of funny deep down inside. Sort of muddy and sticky-like. He shook his head and straightened up.

"Time-out, ump," he said.

"What's the matter, guy," Butch accused. " 'Fraid of me?"

"No, I'm not," Milo said levelly. "But I thought you might like to know that you're using a cracked bat."

Butch stared down at the bat. He saw the crack; then turned to stare at Milo. He scratched his head, puzzled. It seemed to take quite a while for the big third baseman to find words. When he did find them, there was a very different tone in his voice.

"You . . . you didn't have to tell me about that crack," he said. "I . . . I wonder—" he stopped a moment. "I guess I sure do owe you some sort of an apology, Milo."

"No you don't," Milo said.

"I . . . I've been a plenty big sap," Butch said.

"Just get yourself another bat, and let's finish the game," Milo said without looking at him.

"Not me, brother," the third baseman

shook his head. "I've no right to be batting here. Not after . . . boy, oh, boy, how poor a sport can a guy be!" Butch looked as though he wanted to kick himself.

"What goes on here?" the umpire asked. "Let's play ball."

"I . . . I, could I talk to you a minute, ump?" Butch said. "No, I guess maybe I better talk to everybody. Hey, you guys," he shouted. "Come on in here a minute. Everybody."

It wasn't easy for Butch. But no one on either team said a word as he poured out his story about all the unsporting things he had done. Then he was finished and everyone stood around sort of gazing at the ground.

"Well," the umpire said, "this is a little unusual. Just what would you boys like to do about it? After all, the game is tied, but it isn't finished, and—"

"I think the Redwings are the winners," Butch said. "By default or something."

"No, we can't do that," Art Ryan argued.

"Well, how about just forgetting today's game and playing it over again, say, day after tomorrow?" the Otter pitcher suggested.

"That's it," Lefty Lewis agreed. "That's the deal. Start all over."

"Yeah," Butch said. He looked from one player to another, as though hopeful that they wouldn't demand he quit the team. "Even Stephen. Is that all right with you, Milo?"

"Even Stephen?" Milo said. "Sure, that's great with me." He liked the new friendly look that was in the Otter third baseman's eyes. It could be that Butch had a different view of things now.

"Shake?" Butch Carson put out his hand.

Milo took it in a firm grip. "Shake!" he said.

Then they stood grinning at each other. Everything was even Stephen, all over.